waiting for normal

waiting for normal

leslie connor

Katherine Tegen Books
An Imprint of HarperCollins Publishers

Library of Congress Cataloging-in-Publication Data

Connor, Leslie.

Waiting for normal / Leslie Connor. — 1st ed.

p. cm.

Summary: Twelve-year-old Addie tries to cope with her mother's erratic behavior and being separated from her beloved stepfather and half-sisters when she and her mother go to live in a small trailer by the railroad tracks on the outskirts of Schenectady, New York.

ISBN 978-0-06-089088-9 (trade bdg.)

ISBN 978-0-06-089089-6 (lib. bdg.)

[1. Family problems—Fiction. 2. Mothers—Fiction. 3. Stepfathers—Fiction. 4. Friendship—Fiction. 5. Self-reliance—Fiction. 6. Schenectady (N.Y.)—Fiction.] I. Title.

PZ7.C7644Wai 2008   2007006881

[Fic]—dc22   CIP
                                                              AC

Typography by Jennifer Heuer

2 3 4 5 6 7 8 9 10

❖

First Edition

163 - 0221

Marley, this one is for you.

contents

tin box on a tar patch

Maybe Mommers and I shouldn't have been surprised; Dwight had told us it was a trailer even before we'd packed our bags. But I had pictured one of those parks—like up on Route 50. I thought trailers were always in *trailer parks*. I expected a little grass patch out front, daisy-shaped pinwheels stuck into the ground, one of those white shorty fences and a garden gnome.

Dwight crossed traffic and pulled the truck up over the curb. When he stopped, Mommers' head bumped against the window. "What are we doing here?" she asked. I watched Dwight's face for the answer. Dwight is my stepfather. Well, he's really my *ex*-stepfather since he and Mommers split for good. That was two years ago. (It's best to know right from the beginning that my family is hard to follow—like a road that keeps taking twists and turns.) But Dwight had always told me, there'll be no "ex" between you and me, Addie, girl, and I believed him.

"I *said*, what are we doing here?" Mommers repeated.

"This is the place," Dwight mumbled.

Mommers sat up. She opened her eyes wide and looked out the front windshield. Then she screamed. "Dwight! You've got to be kidding me! This is the *city*!"

Dwight leaned away from her—protecting his ear—and in that quiet way he's got about him, he told Mommers, "Come on, Denise. Let's not go over it again. You know this is all I've got left. You can move in here, or go to Jack's place." He slid out of the truck.

Mommers swung her door open so hard it came back at her. She kicked it and it whined on the hinge. "I can't live with Jack!"

She was talking about my grandfather on my father's side. I call him Grandio. That's his grandpa name, which my father taught me to say a long time ago. That's about all my father had time to teach me; he died when I was barely three. I've always kind of felt as if my father *gave* me

Grandio—or tried to anyway—that he left him to me so I'd have as much family as possible. Thing is, he kind of left Grandio to Mommers, too. I've never seen two people who wanted less to do with each other.

"I hate Jack!" Mommers hollered at Dwight. "And I hate you!"

"I know," said Dwight, as if he had accepted that a long time ago.

I unfolded myself from the back of the cab, where I'd been squashed in the little jump seat, and slipped down to the ground. Dwight lifted our bags out of the back of his truck and handed Mommers a key.

"Go in and have a look. We can work on it some if you want," he said. "And the computer is in for you and Addie." He tried to say all this with a hopeful note in his throat—Dwight always did that.

But Mommers threw the key down hard as she could. It hit the ground with a tiny ringing sound like a little chime. "I suppose you want me to over-flow with gratitude!" she yelled. "I get a cruddy tin box for a house and a dinosaur for a computer! Lucky me! What about the duplex, Dwight? You could have given me that!"

"The duplex is gone to pay for the house, Denise." Dwight kept his lips in a line. Mommers kicked at her own overstuffed suitcase. Then she said all kinds of other things I won't mention, but boy, did I hear some language.

Dwight walked away from her. That might have seemed mean to anyone who happened to be watching that day, but I didn't really blame him. He had my little sisters to think of—half sisters, that is. They're Dwight's kids. I'm not. (Like I said, my family is full of twists and turns.) He leaned down and gave me a shaky hug. I squeezed him back and swallowed hard. He whispered into my shoulder. "I'm sorry, Addie, girl." Then he looked at me eye to eye and said, "I'll be around—you know that."

I nodded. "And you'll bring Brynna and Katie, right?"

"Of course. As often as I can."

"Then it'll be all right," I said, and I faked a big old smile.

Dwight got back into his truck and raised a hand to wave good-bye. He turned his wheels away from us and with a screech and a lurch, he

4

was outta there.

I stood next to Mommers, both of us looking at the trailer. The thing was dingy and faded. But I could tell that it'd once been the color of sunshine. It was plunked down on a few stacks of cinder blocks at the corner of Freeman's Bridge Road and Nott Street in the city of Schenectady—in the state of New York. It was a busy corner—*medium* busy, I'd say. The only patch out front was the tarry blacktop bubbling up in the heat of the late summer afternoon. No pinwheels. No garden gnome.

"Can you believe this, Addison?" Mommers said. She stared at the trailer door. "That reprobate."

"*Reprobate?*" I said. "There's one for my vocabulary book."

"Yeah, Addie. And for the definition, you just write *Dwight*!"

She fell into a heap and started to cry. I stooped beside Mommers. I gave her shoulder a pat, tried to get her to look at me, but she wouldn't. Then the little flash of silver caught my eye. I reached down and picked up the key.

small stuff

I've always sort of liked small places like tents and bunk beds. You can make them all your own just by being there to fill up the space. I rolled the key over in my palm. I wanted to see the inside of that trailer.

I climbed the metal steps—pretty sturdy—and stuck the key into the lock. I gave it a twist. Suddenly, there was such noise! The rushing and whooshing filled my ears, and my legs went weak underneath me. The key quivered in the lock of the trailer.

"Yah!" I jumped off the step and started to run back to Mommers. "It's starting up!" I yelled. The loud clack-clack-clacking noise at my back drowned me out. Mommers covered both her ears, her mouth wide open in a silent scream. She had big round eyes fixed on something over my head. I was sure the trailer was falling off its blocks—about to crash. I turned in time to see the blur; a silver train streaked by on the tracks right above our new home.

Silence followed. Then Mommers wailed, "We're living *under* a train!"

"Well, sort of *in front of*," I said, glancing back at the empty tracks. My heart was still pounding.

"What's the difference?" she said.

I braved the metal stairs again, took a breath and pulled open the door to the trailer.

It really *was* a little house inside—more of a home than one of those camper things, and it wasn't going anywhere unless something came to get it; there was no steering wheel. I had to laugh about that when I thought of Mommers and me standing outside screaming all because a train was going by.

"Look at the kitchen," I said to Mommers. "Isn't it perfect?" She rolled her eyes at me. It was kinda shrimpy, like it was made for sixth-graders instead of grown-ups, but that made me smile. I'd be starting sixth grade in about a week. I flipped a light switch and a bare bulb came on above the sink. Mommers squinted.

"How classy," she mumbled.

"Hey, look," I said. "Everything is six steps." I counted out six baby steps from the front door. That put me right at the kitchen sink. I counted six more and that put me in the living room, which was also the dining booth *and* had an extra sleeping bed. In a pinch, we could drop the table down and cover it with the seat cushions. Six more steps and I stood in front of the bedroom, the only real bedroom.

"This one's yours, Mommers."

"Wow," she said, "I get a folding door. And a window with a view of—what the heck is that? A Laundromat?" She let a sigh buzz through her lips. "I got me a regular Luxury Suite. Oh, and it's near the bathroom. What more could I want?" She tossed her splitting suitcase onto her new bed. Her elbow hit the doorjamb and she muffled a swear.

I didn't mind Mommers getting the Luxury Suite. I got the bunk tucked up high, way at the other end of the trailer. I climbed up the ladder— six rungs, by the way—and pushed open the curtain on a string to try it out. I straightened up on my knees, inched a little higher and let my head thunk the ceiling a few times. I fell down giggling.

I put my nose to the little square window and looked out onto the tar-patch yard and out to the steep, grassy bank that led up to the train tracks. Meadow flowers grew on the slope, the same kind I'd seen growing out at Grandio's farm fields across Freeman's Bridge.

I turned and pulled the curtain shut across my bunk. Then I poked my head out. "Look, Mommers, I have my own sleeping cupboard!"

She looked over her shoulder. "Looks like a chintzy mattress on top of a closet and a dresser to me," she said.

"There's a closet?" I tipped my head down to see below my bed and almost flipped out of the bunk.

Mommers let out a tiny laugh. "You like it here, don't you?"

I climbed down and crawled into the closet. I tucked up my knees and looked out toward the minikitchen, grinning. "It's not bad," I said. "I like small stuff. I'll make dinner tonight."

Mommers went to get settled into the Luxury Suite. I pushed up my sleeves and got to work in the kitchen.

Out on Freeman's Bridge Road the cars and trucks bumped and rumbled over the rough pavement while Mommers and I ate our first trailer supper—macaroni and cheese with peas—from the groceries Dwight had left for us. Mommers leaned on her elbow and looked out the front window. I saw her sniffle into her napkin once or twice.

"I'm going to see if that old computer still works," she said after dinner.

"I'll do the dishes," I said.

She turned on her computer and soon she was on the Internet.

"Pretty nice Dwight gave us the computer. And the *Internet*, too," I added. "Are you on the Web?"

"I'm just looking for a chat," Mommers said.

I did the dishes as perfectly as I could. I dried them and put each one away in the little cupboards. I wanted us to keep this new place nice.

The cleaning had gotten away from us when we'd had the house. Dwight had tried. He would come home from work and start the laundry and drag out the vacuum. The Littles—that's what Dwight and I called my little sisters whenever we were talking about both of them at once—and I would scrub bathrooms or roll socks. We'd pick up the toys, stack Mommers' magazines and empty her ashtrays. But after Dwight moved out, the place got bad. Really bad. Mommers was never up at breakfast time and I left a lot of mess from making toast for the Littles. (I was always running late for the school bus.) We used napkins instead of plates and that helped some. But then we couldn't keep up with the trash. Picker's Waste Removal quit stopping for our cans because the bill didn't get paid. That's one of the things Dwight didn't like.

Now, with just the two of us, there weren't so many dishes. I finished them up quickly. As small as the trailer was, I didn't know where I should be that night. New places always do that to me. Even when I was little, when Mommers married Dwight and we moved into his house, I'd wandered from room to room like I had to try on each one, get it to fit. Soon Brynna was born and later Katie. Eventually, we were all right at home there, all filling up the space. But that was a long time ago.

"Addie! You're pacing!" Mommers wagged one arm behind her to shoo me away. "Do you need to pee?" She laughed and scooted closer to her keyboard and typed.

I laughed too. But I knew she was done talking to me for the night. She was absorbed in her computer chat. I went up into my cupboard with a book.

That first night, as I lay on my chintzy mattress, I listened to the sounds outside—the cars and trucks and especially the trains. I wondered what Brynna and Katie were doing. They'd be asleep, of course, or should be. I pictured Katie's pink fist curled next to her mouth, Brynna's cheek resting on her folded hands. I thought of Dwight filling up the bedroom doorway with all his height. "Are they out, Addie?" he'd ask. I'd whisper back, "Been gone for an hour." Then I'd reach up a hand and catch the kiss he'd blow me and tuck my fist under my own pillow before sleeping. I caught a pretend kiss there in the trailer. I wanted to keep them all close.

I woke in the night to the rumble and clack, and to Mommers slamming her fist down on the table and swearing about the noise. I opened my eyes and saw her leaning toward the bluish light of her computer screen. I drifted back to sleep wondering when the train would come again, and if it would be a passenger train singing by, or a freighter clacking and swaying. But a few nights later I was done waking for the trains. Me, I'm good at getting used to things—been doing it all my life.

welcome pie

Across the street from the trailer was what I called the Empty Acre. (I don't know if it really was a whole acre, but I was just talking to myself anyway.) It was a big parking lot of potholes that no cars ever bothered to fall into because there was no reason to drive through there anymore. The old Big N store at the back of the lot was empty too, though Mommers said you used to be able to get your discounts and your hoagie sandwich there. (A hoagie is the same as a submarine sandwich, or a poor-boy, or a hero or a grinder, depending on where you come from—or in my case, where your parents come from. Mommers had grown up in Ohio, and that's where they call it a hoagie.)

At the front of the Empty Acre was the filling station and minimart. On my way home from my first day of school I discovered a big glass apartment that looked like a greenhouse off the back of the store. It jutted out with a long sloping roofline that nearly met the bumpy pavement. The leaves of plants and trees pressed themselves against the inside of the glass. But I could also see colors and fabrics and bamboo furniture inside. Somebody definitely lived there.

I went right into the minimart that afternoon to scope things out. It's good to know your neighbors. Funny thing about the corner—it had more businesses than residences. In fact, pretty early on I figured out I was *it*—the one kid living where Nott Street crossed Freeman's Bridge Road.

I checked out the shelves in the minimart—everything from marshmallows and onion soup mix to sunglasses and disposable diapers. Amazing what a little store can hold. I walked around the coffee counter and noted the doughnut case, the microwave and the minifreezer full of ice cream bars and quick snacks. A man pushed past me to slap a beef and bean burrito into the microwave. I smelled cigarettes on him—a different brand from Mommers', but just as bad. I closed off my nose from the inside and took my next breath through my mouth.

"Late lunch, Mick?" A woman's voice sang out over the hum of the oven. I turned and caught my first glimpse of Soula. She was sitting on a lawn chair just a few feet behind me. I had missed her while I was busy looking at all the food and trying not to smell the burrito guy. Soula blended in with the displays, the ones that sell suntan oil and camera film and announce chances to win trips to Hawaii. She looked like an enormous plastic doll in a big flowered party dress. Of course, there wasn't any possible way Soula would have fit into a *small* dress, but this one billowed. A pair of pink plastic flip-flops matched her toenail polish. She was a perfect fit for that glass apartment out back, and I thought to myself, It has to be hers.

"Hey, Soula!" The burrito guy nickered back at her. "How ya feeling?"

"Good today," she told him. She touched the sides of her black hair like she was adjusting a hat. "Four down and four to go," she told the guy. She winked a perfectly lined eye at him.

Four *whats*? I wondered.

A skinny man at the register spoke. "Don't let her fool you, Mick. She's a terrible patient." He filled a see-through bin in front of him with match-books and smiled knowingly at Soula.

"Don't be ratting me out, now, Elliot."

"Be good to yourself and I won't." He grinned and shook a finger at her.

They laughed as Mick paid for his food. As soon as he was out the door, Soula tapped her foot out in front of her and asked, "So what do you know, Little Cookie?" She was looking straight at me.

I gulped. "Uh . . . well, I know you're Soula and he's Elliot." I offered. "And that was Mick with the burrito. And he's a smoker. I'm kind of a snoop," I admitted.

They laughed hysterically. I looked back and forth between them. Elliot's head was back, his mouth wide open. He had a golden filling in one tooth and it matched the little hoop earring in his left lobe. His skin was all freckles on freckles, even up into his short red hair. I didn't think I'd been that funny, but maybe they were just looking for a reason to laugh, the way some people do.

"And who are you?" he finally asked.

"Addison Schmeeter," I said. "Or just Addie."

"You like your new place across the way, Addie?" Soula asked.

I nodded. It was nice to know I'd been noticed. "We were a little surprised," I said. "The train, I mean." Again they laughed, and so did I when I realized they'd probably watched us move in. Soula dabbed her eyes and pulled her bright pink lips into an O around her teeth like she was trying to stop laughing. She shook out a few more chuckles in spite of herself. "But I like this corner," I said. "It's got just about everything a person needs when ya think about it. I figure this minimart covers everything except the laundry, and the Laundromat's right next door to me. By the way, do you know why it's called the Heads and Roses Laundry Stop? What's with the mannequin heads and the plastic roses in the front window?" I asked.

"Well . . ." Elliot cocked his head. "The place is owned by the Roses, as in *Mr*. and *Mrs*. Rose. As for the mannequin heads . . ." He winked at Soula. "All we can figure is, why not?" For the third time, they burst out laughing, and that made me laugh too.

Finally, Soula settled down to a giggle. "Don't mind us, Little Cookie. We just love a good chuckle. And you're right. This corner does have it covered. And if you need something, all you have to do is ask. Now, pick out a pocket of Welcome Pie," she told me.

"Welcome Pie?"

"That's right." Soula pointed to the glass case next to the microwave. "Pick one and give it a spin in the micro-nuker."

"Apple's the best," Elliot said.

"I didn't bring any money," I said.

Soula winked at me with her perfectly lined eye. "It's on us. Welcome to the neighborhood, Cookie."

according to webster's

Mommers asked, "So who's the fat woman?" She'd watched me cross Freeman's Bridge Road.

"That's Soula," I told her. "I stopped by there today right after school to say hello. She gave me this—for free." I bit into the apple pie pocket. The filling squeezed out the sides and I wolfed another bite to catch it before it dripped.

"Disgusting," Mommers mumbled.

The warm apple goo ran a trail between my fingers. I licked it.

Mommers' bathrobe hung open over a dingy T-shirt. Her hair was pressed flat on one side—sticking straight out on the other. Her mascara was smeared below both eyes and she drummed her fingernails against a can of diet cola. It was four o'clock in the afternoon and she'd just gotten up.

"Anyway, Soula lives out back of the shop. I saw the place. It's called the Greenhouse and it looks like one, too. Full of plants. She said welcome to the neighborhood," I told Mommers.

"Some neighborhood," she mumbled.

"It's not bad," I said. "Anyway, what are we having for dinner tonight?"

"Dinner?" She shrugged. "I just woke up."

I watched Mommers sit down in front of the old computer. She lit a cigarette and waited for the online service to connect. "This thing's a piece of junk." She tapped her finger hard on the mouse. "Addison, I don't want you hanging around that stinking gas station like some poor little puppy, hear?"

"Uh-huh," I said. But already I was thinking that I would anyway. I liked Soula and Elliot, and I liked the apple pie pocket.

Mommers mumbled something else about fumes and poor health.

I fanned the cigarette smoke and raised an eyebrow at her—something I do very well.

She said, "Oh don't start." But then she laughed a little and gave me a sideways grin.

I loved it whenever I could get a laugh like that

out of Mommers. In those couple of seconds, our lives seemed normal.

I sat up in my bunk to write in my vocabulary notebook. Mommers had started me on it after she saw a TV show on helping kids enrich their language skills. See, she had the Love of Learning. I didn't. She had said my father didn't have it either, and that's what had really got between them and wrecked their marriage. I don't know if she was exactly right about all of that. Like I said, my father didn't live long enough to leave me with much for memories. But Grandio always said that his son was a genius, especially when it came to machines. My father loved making things go. He died racing cigarette boats out on the Mohawk River—that's the river that flows beneath Freeman's Bridge.

If my daddy was a genius, it didn't rub off on me. I have a terrible time with school stuff. But Mommers always says that if you just *pretend* to be smart people will believe that you are. Long after she'd stopped caring about the vocab book, I kept it going because I figured she was right. I liked it best when I could get the definitions from a real person. Webster's dictionary confused me, and alphabetical order drove me nuts.

I wrote *mortgage* first because I'd been meaning to get that one down for a while—ever since we'd moved into the trailer. Dwight had told me what it was. *Mortgage* is what you pay back to the bank when you have borrowed money from them to buy a house. It's a deal you make and you have to stick to it. The money to pay the mortgage came from Dwight, and that is the money Mommers used on something that wasn't the mortgage. (It was kind of the same as what happened to the money for Picker's Waste Removal.) The bank took back Dwight's house, which meant the deal was ruined, and that's why we had to leave. Of course, Dwight had moved out long before that. Mommers asked him for a divorce. He didn't want that, but he finally gave in. We stayed at his house until Mommers messed up—big-time. After all the court stuff, Katie and Brynna moved in with Dwight since he was their natural daddy.

When the judge decided my sisters should live with Dwight, I knew it was going to change my life. I bet my name never even came up in that courtroom. But the decision meant I'd soon change my address, my school, my friends, and worst of all, the shape of my family. Twist and turn.

Reprobate is what I wrote next, and of course I knew the definition wasn't really *Dwight* like Mommers had said. And here again was the nightmare of Webster's: Once I finally found *reprobate*, which happened to be at the very bottom of one page, thank you, I forced my eyes to hang on to the teeny tiny letters. But then I had to look up *morally* and *unprincipled*, too. I held a three-by-five card under the words to keep them still. Putting it all together, I decided a reprobate was a low-life loser, a person who didn't follow the rules, which of course wasn't the definition of Dwight at all.

I think Dwight tried the hardest of anybody.

There's that saying about someone's heart being in the right place, and that's why I couldn't blame Dwight for moving Mommers and me into the trailer. He only had one heart and it couldn't be everywhere. He told me, "I can't fix all of it, Addie, so I'm fixing the part I can." I knew by the skin around his eyes turning pink that he could have cried.

"What are you doing tonight, Addie?" Mommers asked suddenly.

"Two entries for the vocab book," I said.

"*Mortgage* and *reprobate*."

She looked up from her keyboard and said, "Hmm. Two words I could have done without this month." She sighed. "Can you use 'em in a sentence?"

I thought for a minute. Anything I came up with was likely to get me in trouble. *I wish my mother hadn't blown the mortgage money. Dwight is the furthest thing from a reprobate that I can imagine.* But it wouldn't have been nice to say those sentences to Mommers. "The mortgage is paid so the bank is happy," I said. "And . . . There is a boy in my class at school who is a reprobate."

Mommers snorted. "For real? There's a jerk in your class?"

I nodded. "He stepped on his ice-cream sandwich in the lunchroom. Then he offered it to me as a welcome-to-your-new-school present."

Mommers leaned closer to her computer screen. "Yep, that's a reprobate."

"I thought it was too bad about the ice cream," I said. "People shouldn't wreck perfectly good food."

"Hmm. Hey, do you have homework?"

"First day. There isn't any."

"What about flute?"

"Yep," I said. "I'm going to do that now."

Funny to stink at something and still love it. If there is one thing worse than rows of letters on a page it has to be rows of musical notes. You can't steady them with a three-by-five card when you need all your fingers to key with. Mostly, I played by ear.

What I really wanted was to play the *piccolo*. But you have to learn the flute first. So far, I'd stuck with it. Now that we'd moved, I had a new problem; we had basically *stolen* the flute from my last school. I was assigned a school instrument. I was allowed to keep the flute over the summer so I could practice. But the flute should have gone back to Borden School once we knew we were moving. Now I got a wave of uneasiness every time I looked at the little black case.

I'd already met the music teacher at my new school. Her name was Ms. Rivera. She said she would be trying out all the new students in the next week or two. Then she'd let us know about our placements for school lessons. I was nervous about that because I knew I'd have to explain to her that I didn't have the Love of Learning.

the over-underpass

I couldn't decide what to call the thing the train went by on. It was either an overpass or an underpass. Maybe it depended on where you were standing. Even Webster's couldn't help me out because Webster's didn't have all the details. The overpass part had a purpose; the train was on it. So probably that was the most right word. The under-pass part was not used anymore—kind of like the Empty Acre. Soula told me, "That road used to be the main way in to our intersection. Then the city rerouted the traffic. See, the old way skirts a brown field," she said as she pointed across the road. "That's a big old polluted spot on the earth, Little Cookie. It happens when an industry leaves and won't clean up after itself. It stinks." Soula posted newspaper clippings about that, and other things that had to do with the city—especially the area near our corner—on a board near the entrance to the minimart. I never spent much time reading the postings because newspapers were hard for me to read and I would have felt stupid standing there holding my three-by-five card underneath every line. But I always looked at the pictures.

Anyway, even though nothing went under it anymore, I thought it was important to remember the underpass part. You can't ignore history. I called it the Over-Underpass.

Dwight came on the first Saturday and he brought Brynna and Katie with him. It was raining pretty hard and he rushed them into the trailer. The Littles wiggled like puppies from me to Mommers and back again. If they'd had tails, they'd have wagged them. We just kept hugging one another, which is a good thing for a trailer full of people to do. Mommers kept pulling Katie onto her lap and tucking her nose into her curls. She said, "Go do your errands, Dwight. You can leave the girls with me."

"No thanks," Dwight said.

Mommers sighed—a crying sort of sigh. "They're *my* girls, Dwight! What am I gonna do?

Leave town with 'em? I don't even have a car!"

"Let's just stick to the plan," Dwight said in his quiet way.

"Let the state decide what we do with *our* kids?" Mommers complained. She pushed her coffee cup away and balled up her napkin.

He saw me watching them, listening to them. He pulled in a deep breath and closed his eyes. "That's enough, Denise. Okay?"

We ate the doughnuts Dwight had brought. I made microwave cocoas even though the day outdoors was hot and steamy. It stopped raining at about eleven and Dwight said he'd take us all outside.

"Oh yeah, great idea," Mommers said. "The yard here is so nice for children." She switched on her computer.

Katie and Brynna and I played ghosts in the steam that rose from the broken pavement. I showed them how to pop the tar bubbles with their thumbs. We jumped up and ran from the hot water that squirted out of the rain-filled bubbles. Dwight checked a few things that had to do with the trailer—the power hookup, which we got from the Heads and Roses Laundry Stop next door, and the propane tank that fueled our stove. Then he grabbed a coil of rope from his truck. He stood looking at the Over-Underpass for a second. "I've been thinking . . . there must be a way to put up a swing here."

"Yeah! Yeah!" we cried, and we followed him out to the mouth of the closed-off road where the weeds came up through the cracks in the blacktop. We watched Dwight climb up the crisscrossing metal bars into the belly of the Over-Underpass. We blinked to keep the rusty chips from falling down into our eyes. He looked like a spider-guy all upside down, appearing and disappearing in the shadows. He grunted and threw the looped rope over a steel girder. "How am I doin', girls?" His voice echoed and we cheered him on. Finally, he shimmied down the rope, grinning and sweaty, one arm stretched way out in celebration.

At first the swing had problems. The big knot in the bottom wasn't very comfortable after a few rides, and Katie wasn't strong enough to grab it with her feet. But the next week, Dwight brought a round of wood—all sanded smooth and with a hole drilled in the center. He threaded the rope and knotted it twice under the new seat.

"There it is, girls! The best rope swing ever!" he boomed.

After that, it was the first thing Brynna and Katie wanted to do when they visited. As I pulled Brynna back and let her fly away and return to me for the next several Saturdays, I thought the best part about the swing was the way Dwight had said, "There it is, girls!" He'd made me feel like I was one of his girls too.

a renovation

The hard part came when Dwight got a renovating job up in Lake George. I knew something was changing when he came in looking so serious. He took Mommers outside to talk. I climbed into my bunk and watched and listened at the little square window.

"You could have given me some warning!" she screamed.

"I tried to get through for hours. You must have been online, Denise. I'm sorry about this, but I gotta take the job. It's a chance to catch up on a lot of bad bills. I found good day care for the babies—"

My heart took a dive. Of course—Brynna and Katie were going away too.

"They need their mother!" Mommers hollered. "You *want* to take them away from me! You have

32

always wanted this! You and Jack did this together, didn't you?"

She meant Grandio. Mommers was no longer on speaking terms with him, which was actually an improvement in their relationship. All they'd ever done was argue.

"No, and I don't *want* this." Dwight shook his head. "But it's the only way, for now. I'll get here every other week. Sundays probably. I'll figure it out."

"Oh, at least be honest, Dwight. You're enjoying this!"

Dwight lost it. "Know what, Denise? I might enjoy it if it weren't for Addie. I hate splitting the girls up!" Then he swore at Mommers—I'd never heard him do that before.

She flew at him—fists pounding—and Dwight grabbed her wrists and turned her. He held on to her, close and hard, so she couldn't hit anymore. She thrashed like a giant fish. The back of her head smashed his lip. He sucked back the blood. He held on, not speaking. Finally, Mommers went limp in his arms. Dwight whispered, "I'm sorry, I'm sorry." They stood there like they were stuck together for a long while. Then Mommers turned and wiped her face on his T-shirt. He handed her his handkerchief and the little black comb from the back pocket of his jeans. She turned her back on him, shook like she was trying to get rid of something, then started pulling the comb through her hair.

Dwight came inside alone. He told me about the move. I didn't admit that I already knew—that I'd listened from my bunk.

He chewed on his fat lip. "I'll get here as often as I can, Addie. But this renovation is gonna be a lot of work. It's an old mansion and the owner wants to turn it into an inn. It's really cool. I want you to see it someday." He let his eyes twinkle for a second. Dwight loved old houses. "But there's a time crunch. I've gotta be done by April."

April! I tried to count the months but I was slow—kind of like the ABC order problem. I just knew it would be most of a year. "I'm not going to see Brynna and Katie. Or you." I let it slip.

"I'll call every week, so we can all talk," he said. "We'll come down every chance we get." He looked as sorry as the time he'd come for Brynna and Katie after the court order.

I tried to cheer up. I didn't want to make him

feel worse. I squeezed my tears away. I took his arm and hugged it close to me. He cupped his other hand on the back of my head. I curled my hands around his forearm and pressed my face into the blond hairs and tanned skin. I always loved Dwight's arms—I don't know why, I just did.

"I'll see you when you can get here," I said, "and Brynna and Katie too."

tryouts and friendships

The flute shook in my hands. I looked up from the piece of music on the stand in front of me. "I can't just play it. Not right off," I said. I waited for Ms. Rivera's response, glad that we were alone. She looked as if I had completely confused her. "I need to hear it first. I need to *know* it," I explained.

"Oh. Well, how many times do you usually need to hear the music before you know it?"

I waited. I knew the answer was at least ten, depending on how long the piece was and how many changes. "Maybe five," I croaked. I cleared my throat. "And I *can* read the music with a note card and hum it to myself. Then I play it back . . . after a few tries, that is. I mean, I can work on it at home." I figured I better stop talking and let poor Ms. Rivera think.

She blinked. "Well, play a piece that you've already mastered," she said.

I closed my eyes and brought the flute to my lips. I played "The Witches' Waltz"—two mini mess-ups along the way but I went on. That was important; you should always go on. I set the flute in my lap and opened my eyes.

"Oh! Lovely!" Ms. Rivera made marks on a try-out sheet. "What a bouncy melody, and you key with a good, light touch, Addison." She thought for a second. "Maybe I can hand you the music ahead of time so you have a chance to assimilate it." She leaned forward and asked, "Do you think that'll work?"

"Yes, thanks. I do."

I let out a big huge sigh on my way back down the hall. *Assimilate*, I thought. I knew what Ms. Rivera had meant because of how she'd used the word but I was going to double-check with Webster's anyway. The tryout was over with. Now all I had to worry about was working hard on the music at home—and the fact that I had a basically stolen flute. I rocked the little instrument case in my hand as I walked.

"Did you go see Rivera?"

I looked into the face of the reprobate boy—the ice-cream sandwich smasher—whose name, I had learned, was Robert. He stood in my way, leaning against the wall outside our classroom. "Yes. I saw her," I said.

"Did you get in?"

"In?"

"Yeah. Stage Orchestra."

"Stage Orchestra?"

"It's for the best musicians," Robert said. "We play at holiday concerts and stuff."

I suddenly realized that was why it was called a *tryout*. "Uh, I'm just doing lessons, I guess."

"Figures," he said. "Well, I'm in. I play the cello."

I didn't bother to tell him that all the cellos I'd ever heard in school sounded like yawning cows or bad gas. Or that I wondered how a little squirt like him could even hang on to a cello. I pushed past him into our classroom.

My new friend Marissa, who was about as small as any sixth-grade girl can be, turned from the computer station and asked softly, "How did it go?"

"Fine," I whispered back. "I didn't know about

38

Stage Orchestra," I added.

Then my other new friend, Helena, who was about as big as any sixth-grade girl can be, looked up from her desk and whispered, "I got in last year for violin. It's really fun. And Ms. Rivera will let you know by Halloween if you make it."

"Not a chance." Robert had put himself right in the middle of our conversation—standing in the way, that is.

"You didn't hear her play. What do you know?" Helena piped.

"I know that you are an amazon!" He puffed himself up to look as big as he could. "And . . ." he boomed.

I cringed. I knew what was coming next. Word had already gotten out.

". . . I know that Nurse Sandi had to give *you* the B.O. talk today. Right after gym class." He pointed to his armpit and pinched his nose. "Ha-ha-ha!"

Helena hid her reddening face.

"Hey!" I said. "Leave her alone, Robert, you *reprobate*!"

Later, I met Helena outside the school and I told her it didn't matter about what Robert said.

"School nurses have all kinds of talks. Remember the 'Don't pick your nose talk' from kindergarten? And the 'Did you eat a good breakfast talk'? I used to get that one twice a week at my other school," I said. "Everybody gets the B.O. talk eventually. Now yours is out of the way. I went through it," I admitted. "My mother told me I smelled. Now I use Fresh Whisper every day."

"Oh," said Helena. "I wish *my* mother had told me. I can't believe I was stinking like that today." We started down Nott Street together. We passed the gate to the college campus and walked past a little Tibetan shop and admired some paper lanterns in the window. Helena would turn off at Seneca Street, where the Goose Hill Barber Shop pole twirled on the corner, and I'd continue down to the minimart—always my first stop after school.

"Don't you hate it all?" I said. "B.O. *and* . . ."— I opened my sweater to one side and took a quick look at my chest—". . . getting boobs?" I figured I could say this to Helena; her boobs were ahead of my boobs. "My puberty book says there's no way to stop 'em." I paused. "Darn things could get *huge*!" I opened my eyes wide.

That made Helena laugh. Helena laughing made

me laugh. As we walked past Hose Company No. 6, two of the firemen who were out front smiled at us. "What's so funny?" one called.

"Nothing!" I called back quickly, but Helena and I looked at each other and cracked up even more. She bent over, holding her stomach. The firefighters started laughing too.

"Why are we laughing?" one wanted to know.

"Don't tell, don't tell!" Helena whispered. She pushed at me.

I shook my head. We continued down the sidewalk in a fit, bouncing off each other as we went.

By the time we reached Seneca Street, we'd recovered enough to speak almost normally again. "Addie, I hope Robert is wrong. I hope you make the Stage Orchestra," said Helena. "We need another good flute in the woodwinds."

I smiled at Helena and decided on the spot that making the Stage Orchestra was one of my new goals.

gates and bridges

"Hey, Soula?"

"Yes, Cookie?"

"What do you know about Onion College?"

"Onion College? You mean *Union* College?"

I closed my eyes and pictured the letters on the sign at the entrance. "Oh yeah. It *is* Union." I laughed and knocked myself in the head with the heel of my hand. "I should have known that!"

Soula laughed. "We all got our gaps. Fine place, so I hear," she said. "Pretty campus, too. I go special to see the Jackson's Garden when the roses bloom in June."

"It looks like there's a different world inside those gates."

"Hmm. Gates'll do that. Just like bridges," Soula said. She bent to pull up the glued flap on a cardboard box. "Wanna help me stack the 'ronis?"

"Sure." I picked up a few boxes of macaroni and began placing them on the shelf.

"Just do them nice so Elliot won't have a chicken when he gets in," Soula warned. I smiled back. Elliot was like that; things had to be neat.

Soula passed me a few more boxes. Her hands were shaking. She stopped still and wiped her brow.

"I'll get these. You sit down," I said.

Soula sighed, reached behind her, and let herself down into the lawn chair. I'd seen her scoot that chair all over the shop, sometimes just walking her big legs into it to move it. It would have been funny if not for the fact that she really *needed* to sit often. I kept thinking about how she'd said, "Four more to go." Soula was sick with something. Mommers had told me that it wasn't nice to ask about people's health problems. "If they want you to know, they'll tell ya," she'd said. So I waited to be told.

"That's better." Soula pushed a grin at me as she settled into her chair. "Thank you, Cookie."

I patted her hand real quick. She fanned her face and blew a puff of her breath through her bright pink lips.

"What do you mean about gates and bridges?" I asked.

"Hmm . . . just that whole passageway feeling. Like there's gotta be something better on the other side."

"Oh," I said. I squared a row of boxes with my hands and went on stacking. "Do you think that's true?"

Soula shrugged. "Probably just a myth. But the human race likes to have things to believe in. Including me. I've always wanted to move over to the other side of Freeman's Bridge. Get out of the city. I've got it in my head that I could get a better life. A safer life," she added.

"Really?"

"Uh-huh. Seems to me that any place where there's more grass and more trees is safer. The city has dangers, you know. Even our little corner here, I'm afraid." Soula stared at the floor ahead of her and was quiet for a moment.

I waited, then asked, "Like the brown fields?"

"Yes, Cookie. And the exhaust and the refuse, the use and misuse and then no use at all. I mean, look out back here." She pointed a thumb toward the Empty Acre and shook her head. "What can you do with a cement field full of holes? Waste, waste, waste. And here I am, selling junk food outta the micro-nuker, cigarettes, gasoline by the tankful! Talk about waste! I'm part of it too."

"Hmm. But you know, Soula, I've got a grandpa and he lives across the bridge and up on a farm. He's got an orchard and a vegetable garden and I guess he's healthy." I thought for a second. "But he's kind of a grump. Like he isn't any happier for living there."

"No?" she said. A little smirk came loose at one corner of her mouth.

I shook my head. "I know the health stuff is important, but I think there's more to getting happy than that."

She leaned forward, kind of studying me. I worried that I shouldn't have said it. Soula actually might have been happy just to have good health.

"I think you need heroes, too," I said. I made a little fist for punch.

"Heroes?" she asked. "Like friends and family?"

"They *can* be friends or family," I said. "Webster's says—"

"Webster's?"

"The dictionary," I explained. "A hero is someone

who sets themselves apart from others. You know—someone who is strong or shows courage, takes a risk. And I know Webster's is probably talking about well-known heroes. Like from the newspapers and history books. Inventors and athletes and people like Martin Luther King."

"Uh-huh." Soula was still listening.

"But don't you think it's possible . . ."—I twisted up my face—". . . that every person is a hero to someone else?" I said.

Soula sat back. She blinked at me once and said, "Well, Little Cookie, I guess you could be right. Never thought of it myself."

"Never thought of what?" Elliot asked as he came through the door. He paused at the cash counter, running one hand through his close red hair and straightening the Quick-Pick sign with his other.

"Heroes," Soula answered. "Addie says we've all got 'em."

"Hope so." Elliot grinned. "Makes living kinda scary, otherwise."

The three of us looked at one another for a second or two. I did a double thumbs-up in agreement. Then Soula and Elliot each put up two thumbs with me.

"Six thumbs up," I said. "You can't beat that!"

tv and toast dinners

"Is there dinner?" I asked.

Mommers flapped a hand at me to make me be quiet.

"My homework's done and I already practiced."

"I heard, I heard," Mommers mumbled. She typed furiously and squinted at the computer screen. She read something and typed again.

"So, do you want me to cook?"

No answer.

Truth was I never really liked dinnertime. Breakfast was our best meal because it was the only meal that was normal. What I mean by that is we had either toast or cereal. That's normal for breakfast—everyone eats those things for breakfast. But *we* often had cereal or toast for dinner, too.

I discovered that if I just added tomato and melted cheese to the toast it looked much more like dinner. And if I just heated up a can of condensed soup—tomato or cream of chicken, for example—and didn't add the water, it tasted pretty good poured over toast. So, toast dinners became my specialty.

Mommers cooked too. There were nights when something seemed to take hold of her and she'd cook up a storm, making quarts of spaghetti sauce and homemade garlic bread. She'd throw the noodles at the fridge to see if they'd stick and then call me to the table, and we'd eat and eat as if we were bears packing it away for winter. I remembered a time back at the house when she'd roasted a turkey in the middle of July and she'd made the gravy and mashed potatoes. She'd called Dwight at work and had him stop for cranberry sauce. We had Thanksgiving in July out at the picnic table.

But most nights at the trailer, Mommers was not interested in dinner—not in cooking it anyway. Then I'd scrounge around in the minikitchen—Mommers was not a good grocery shopper—and make something up. Often we'd agree that this meal or that meal hadn't come out too great. But there were other things besides the food that could ruin dinner.

Mommers liked to watch the TV and surf the Net at the same time. If she looked at the TV too long, the Internet kicked her off and then she got mad. Sometimes that ruined dinner. And on this night she tuned in her favorite show: *Jeanette for the Judgment,* which was always on at seven o'clock—dinnertime.

I hated *Jeanette for the Judgment.*

"See that, Addison?" Mommers said. "I always make the same decision as Jeanette. I could've done that job." She inched forward in her chair.

"I wouldn't wanna be Jeanette," I said. I cut two pieces of toast into squares, poured some cream of chicken soup over them and set the plate down in front of Mommers.

"Why?" Mommers asked. She did not look away from the TV.

"She doesn't know what she's doing," I said. "I mean, she can never be sure." I looked at Jeanette up there in her black robe and my stomach got all nervous. I couldn't watch. The bad thing about the trailer was there was no way to get away from that show.

"Watch this, Addie," Mommers said, pointing to the set. "See, the woman owned the catering company before she became partners with the pastry chef. He's the little guy with curly hair and . . ."

I didn't want to care about the caterer or the pastry chef. I squeezed my eyes shut. "Even the person Jeanette rules in favor of isn't gonna really feel good when it's over," I said.

"Why do you say that?" Mommers asked.

"Because they *still* had the fight in the first place," I answered. I finished making up my own plate.

"Look at Jeanette," Mommers said. She shook her head adoringly at the woman on the TV screen. "She is gonna skewer that little sleaze. Just watch!" We waited silently while the verdict came down. "See, I knew it! I knew it!" Mommers let out a yell. "I was right again!"

"You're very good at being Jeanette," I told her.

Maybe if I'd had the Love of Learning, I'd have understood why it was such a good show. But I crawled into my bunk with my plate and closed my curtain. The second case would be presented right after the commercials. I ate my toast dinner, plugging my ears between bites and humming my new flute music while I chewed. I didn't have to hear anything that Jeanette or Mommers decided about those poor people on the TV.

a gift of cream and honey

"Hello!" I waved my arm over my head so hard my shoulder ached.

"Hey, Addie! Come see what we've got in the truck," Dwight called.

I jumped down the trailer steps and headed across the tar-patch yard. Brynna and Katie leaned close to Dwight from either side. All three of them were trying to hide smiles. The Littles each rubbed their faces against Dwight as if they could somehow wipe those grins off on his jeans. They had a secret, and I felt a little bad that I wasn't in on it.

But October had come and I was one month closer to having them all back near me. Dwight's renovation project was on schedule so far, and I figured I could stand it if they wanted to come surprise me every once in a while.

"What's up?" I asked.

"We picked out something special for you," Brynna said.

"Guess what it is, Oddie." Katie jumped up and down. "You want it!"

I peeked into the bed of the truck, where a few canvas tarps were heaped over a lumpy something-or-other.

"We got enough dirty laundry around here," I said.

Dwight flashed his white teeth at me. The Littles giggled.

"Guess, guess!" Katie pleaded.

I took her hand and began to swing it in mine. "Well, let's see. Is it a Christmas tree?"

"No!" More giggles.

"A snowman?"

"No, no, no!"

"Let's see. Halloween is two weeks away. Must be a . . . *pumpkin*!"

"Not just a *pumpkin*," Brynna said. She swung her shoulders from side to side, still full of their secret.

Dwight pulled back the canvas cover. There was a pumpkin, but nestled beside it was a small wire cage.

"Oh, Dwight. What is it?" I asked.

"Ham-pister! Ham-pister!" Katie yanked on my arm as she jumped up and down. "We got you a ham-pister!"

"She means a hamster," Brynna added.

"I don't believe it!" I said. "It's really mine?"

Dwight lifted the cage out of the truck and handed it to me. A little pink nose tunneled up out of the wood chips. Then a pair of black eyes blinked open and out wiggled my own cream and honey–colored hamster.

"Wow!" I whispered. "Thanks, you guys!"

"It's a girl one. What you gonna call it, Oddie?" Katie asked.

"I have to think about that," I said. "I want to give it just the right name."

Mommers met me coming in the door. "Oh yuck!" she said.

"I'll keep her out of your way," I promised, holding the cage to my chest.

"Oh Mommers, she's so cute!" Brynna swooned.

"Ham-pister!" Katie shouted again.

"Katie, it's *hamster*," Brynna said patiently. "There is no *P* in it."

"If there's no pee in that thing, I'll eat my hat," Mommers said. She turned to Dwight, who had come in behind us carrying the pumpkin. "This is lovely, Dwight." Mommers fixed a look on him and gestured toward the cage with her cigarette. "Where are we supposed to put it? In the fridge? Look at this place!" She blew a puff of smoke away from Katie, who was hugging her hip, then took another drag.

Dwight gave her a nod. "So, Denise. How's the job hunt going?"

Mommers sneered at him. "Ha-ha," she said.

"The girls want to go out for lunch. We could find a diner," he said. "That sound good to you?"

"Are you *inviting* me?" Mommers asked.

"Of course. This is your time with them."

So we ate at a place called Numbskull Dorry's Pretty Good Pub Food. Crazy name, but I didn't think about it much at the time. I was nervous going in there. Mommers seemed like a walking grenade around Dwight, and I hated to leave my new hamster at home. But I wanted to make everything go as smoothly as possible so I let myself be herded into a booth with the rest. Mommers sat on one side with Katie and Brynna glued to either side

54

of her, and I sat next to Dwight. "Addie, you are getting so tall." He tilted his head sideways as he looked at the top of my head.

"That's not all she's getting," Mommers said. She winked at me. I squirmed and raised an eyebrow at her. Dwight cleared his throat.

"Everybody know what they want?" he asked. We focused on the menus and nobody said anything more about me, thank heavens.

"I'm going to call the hamster Piccolo," I offered later. "Kinda goes with one of my dreams. You know, to play the piccolo someday."

"Puh-puh-piccolo!" Katie sang. "There's a P in it!"

The five of us were laughing when our meals came. The restaurant owner himself helped the waitress bring our plates and he set my fish-and-chips down in front of me.

"Enjoy!" he said.

I couldn't help thinking that they might have thought we were just a normal family. I don't think it showed, there in the restaurant, how many twists and turns we'd taken. I leaned into Dwight a little, took a bite of my fish, and did what the restaurant owner said: I enjoyed.

The only bad thing about having a good time is when it's over. Dwight was already talking to Mommers, looking for another day to come down, as I kissed my sisters good-bye.

"Sorry you can't come all to home, Oddie," Katie said.

"All to home?"

"She means to *our* home," said Brynna.

"I'm sorry too." I kissed them both good-bye, then watched them go.

The trailer seemed so quiet that night. I climbed into my bunk, took Piccolo out of her cage and let her explore. She hurried along the back of my bunk with her whiskers twitching. I cupped her in my hands. She sat still enough for me to feel that tiny hum of life inside her. I stroked the butterscotch fur with my thumbs, brought her to my lips and kissed her tiny warm head.

"Welcome all to home," I whispered.

a bunch of numbskulls

The next day, I was looking at the bulletin board at the minimart. Soula had a newspaper clipping from a while back with a picture of the Over-Underpass on it. (In fact, I could see a little corner of our trailer in the picture.) Someone had spray-painted graffiti across the top of the Over-Underpass. I read it out loud. "'DORRY IS A NUMBSKULL.' Hey, Soula, what was this about?" I asked.

She flapped a hand at me and laughed. "Oh, that's a story that went on for a while." She thought for a second. "The words appeared up there one morning in spray paint. Everyone just thought it was a prank, a one-shot. The railroad painted over it. But then, it appeared again, only this time it said, 'DORRY IS *STILL* A NUMBSKULL.'"

"Oh no! Get out!" I laughed.

"Seriously, Cookie. I'm telling you the truth! So the railroad cleaned it up again, and wouldn't you know, a few days went by and the rascal came back and put up 'DORRY WILL *ALWAYS* BE A NUMBSKULL.'" Soula laughed and stamped a plastic sandal on the floor. (Sandals in October seemed funny, but Soula had sort of outsized feet, so that's what she wore.) "Anyway, the railroad was getting sick of cleaning up the mess and they thought the city ought to be putting some effort into looking for the culprit. So there was a bit of discussion between the two, you see."

I nodded. I turned to look back at the article on the wall. The door to the minimart swung open and in walked a man. I knew his face but I couldn't remember from where. Hose Company No. 6? No.

Suddenly it hit me. He was the guy from Numbskull Dorry's—the restaurant owner!

"Hey! Numbskull! Get out!" I said. Then I covered my mouth with my hand. "Oops!" Soula started laughing so hard I had to run and get her lawn chair from the candy aisle.

"Who you calling a Numbskull?" the restaurant

guy called after me. He started to laugh too.

"Sorry! I didn't mean *you are* a numbskull and I didn't mean *get out* of here either," I called as I dragged the chair up.

We got Soula settled and she introduced me to Rick. "You were in the pub yesterday, right?" he asked. He put a finger to his lips and thought for a second. "Fish-and-chips?"

I nodded. "But I don't get it. Are you the one who wrote 'DORRY IS A NUMBSKULL' on the overpass?"

"No!" He threw his head back.

"We were in the middle of the story when you walked in," Soula told him. Together they went on to tell me that after the newspaper ran the articles, there had been some letters to the paper about the graffiti. It turned out that Dorry's family knew all along that her sister had done the "decorating," as Rick called it.

"It just happened that I was ready to open the pub around the same time that all of this was going on," he said. "I had been looking for a name and, well, I figured there was no such thing as negative advertising. You could say I stole it." He shrugged and grinned.

"The pub's great," I said.

"Thank you. It's a grind. Eighteen hours a day. But it's my dream," he added. He checked his watch, then looked at Soula. "Could I leave a message for the love of my life? He'll be in soon, no?"

"That's right," Soula said. "There's a notepad by the register. Cookie, would you mind?"

I brought Rick the notepad and a pencil. He scribbled on it and handed it back to me.

"Soula, good luck later this week." He gave her a little salute. "Sorry to run," he said. "Gotta check in with the chef." He hurried out the door.

I looked at the notepad in my hand.

> *Elliot,*
> *Running late tonight. Can you meet*
> *me at the pub after your shift? Call.*
>
> > *Love you, R.*

I looked at Soula. "Huh?" I said. "I thought Elliot was *your* boyfriend."

She smiled and shook her head. "Best friend. And sometimes hero."

a violent storm

"Addie!" Mommers slammed the trailer door behind her. I poked my head out of my curtain and saw her set a bag of groceries down in the kitchen. "Those pumpkin guts stink out there. Can you get them away from the front door?"

"Sure," I said. "Mommers, look." I had the carved pumpkin up in my bunk and I turned it so she could see the face. Piccolo was climbing around the inside of the hollow. Every so often her head would pop out of an eyehole or appear between the teeth of the grinning jack-o'-lantern. Mommers watched, smiling a little. Then Piccolo bit off a chunk of the pumpkin flesh and stuffed it into her cheek and both Mommers and I laughed out loud.

"You like that rat, don't you?"

I nodded. "I'm taking her over to meet Soula

and Elliot today," I said. "They asked me to."

"You're spending an awful lot of time with those people." Mommers put a new carton of milk in the fridge. "You have a home, you know. Such as it is." She bumped her hip against the refrigerator door to close it.

"You should come meet them," I said.

"I'm not gonna do my shopping at the gas station, thanks," Mommers said. She put a hand on her hip and gave me a serious look. "You need to consider whether they really want you hanging around or if they're just being nice."

They were definitely being nice. There was no doubt about that. But how was I supposed to know if they were *just* being nice? I decided to look for signs that I might be a pain and I decided to start that day. I arrived at the minimart with Piccolo tucked into one of those fishing creel baskets—the kind with the lid. Helena had given it to me after her family had a garage sale.

The minimart was quiet when I walked in. Dead quiet. I called for Soula and Elliot. No answer. I headed back to the Greenhouse. The door was open so I stepped inside. I heard the water running in the bathroom and then Elliot's voice, quiet and steady, saying, "It'll stop. It'll stop."

I walked right up to the open bathroom door and there was Soula on her knees, her large body bent to hug the bowl. I couldn't see her head but she heaved and retched as hard as I had ever seen or heard a person do that. I pressed the creel basket close to my chest.

Elliot wrung a washcloth into the sink. "Just remember, you *will* feel better," he said. He stooped to offer her the cloth. Finally, I saw Soula's head come up just a bit. I caught a breath in my chest. She was completely bald.

I started to back out of the doorway. Elliot turned and we locked eyes.

"I better go," I said.

He nodded. "The hospital called this morning. There was an opening for a treatment and—"

Soula threw an arm back and tugged Elliot's pant leg. "Is that my Cookie?" she said, gasping. "Let her stay. I think it's over."

I was frozen on the outside and screaming on my inside. *What's wrong? What's wrong?* I wanted to know.

Elliot asked Soula if she was still cold. He pulled

a wrap around her shoulders. Finally, she stood but Elliot did not let go of her. He kept one hand tucked into her armpit as he helped her shuffle over to her big round papasan chair.

"God, Elliot," she breathed. She rubbed her head with her hand. "Where did we put my hair?"

"Just a minute. Comfort before vanity," he said. He lifted Soula's big legs onto the ottoman and draped a shawl over her lap. He pushed two pillows in behind her and set one of those vomit trays and a box of tissues on the table next to her. Then he brought the black wig and helped her stretch it over her bare head.

"I'm going to check on things up front if you are set," Elliot said. "Unless of course we've already been robbed blind, that is."

"It'll be fine," Soula said. "They leave the money on the counter."

"You have entirely too much trust in people." Elliot gave her arm a stroke before he left. "You're in charge." He tapped me on the head. I kept a gulp inside.

Soula closed her eyes. She rested for a minute in her nest of pillows. Then, just when I thought she might have gone to sleep, she opened her eyes again.

"You're seeing the worst of it, Cookie." She sighed. "This is cancer. And it stinks."

"Cancer," I said. So that was it. And I remembered that one of Grandio's friends had had treatments that'd made him throw up and lose his hair too. I felt an ache in my heart. Grandio's friend had died.

"It grew in my big breast." Soula breathed rhythmically as she spoke. "Wonder I found it. Old big-as-a-fridge me. They said it was the size of a peach pit. And I let the doctor cut on me. 'Cept I swear he used a spoon." She paused, and it seemed like she ought to shake out one of her chuckles but she let go a tiny, whistling sigh instead. "Anyway, what you see here is the violent storm"—she paused to breathe—"of old Soula reacting to chemotherapy."

I nodded. I should have hugged her, it seemed, but my knees felt locked in place and I still had my arms glued to the creel basket. I just stood by her chair not speaking.

"So, did you bring that little mouse of yours?"

"Hamster," I whispered. "Uh-huh. But I could jus—"

"Love to see him," she said.

"Her," I whispered again. I opened the creel and slipped the sleeping ball that was Piccolo out of the tissue nest. I set her down on Soula's crossed arms. The hamster shook off her sleep, sat back on her haunches and worked her whiskers. Soula managed a chuckle.

"I didn't think I liked these little critters," she said.

I said, "You never met Piccolo."

evening interview

I walked right over the pumpkin guts on my way home. Inside, Mommers was heating some water on the gas stove and it had reached a full boil. She came out of her room all dressed up, hair neat as could be. A purse she hadn't used in months dangled from her wrist.

"Good. You're back. I have a job interview," she said. "How do I look?"

"Great," I said. "I like your hair pinned up. And your makeup looks nice." (No blue eye shadow.) "It's dinnertime," I said. "Weird time for a job interview, isn't it?"

"Well, we figured out this was the best time for both of us. We're meeting at a restaurant." She fiddled with one earring.

"What kind of job?"

"Sales," she said. "Oh, I forgot to put the macaroni on! I was gonna have dinner ready for you. Well, water's boiling. I've gotta get up to Union Street. I can't miss my bus. I don't want this guy to know I don't have a car."

"Okay," I said. "Hey, Mommers?"

"What!" She stepped out of the trailer and I followed her.

"Do you do that breast-checking thing?"

"What? Of course!" She started away. She slipped in the pumpkin mush, caught herself and swore. "Addie! Clean that up!" she yelled over her shoulder.

I ducked inside, put the macaroni in the pot and grabbed the broom. While I swept I wished everything good that I could for Mommers. I wished her up to Union Street in time for her bus. I wished her a seat by the window, and something as tasty as fish-and-chips for dinner. I wished up the best interview ever for Mommers. Then I wished something for myself: I wished Mommers back home before midnight.

waiting for mommers

I shouldn't have tried to wait up, it being a school night and all. But I wanted to hear about Mommers' meeting and, well, I just wanted to know she was home. The clock on the microwave read 11:45. Piccolo was busy running on her wheel—it squeaked just a bit with every turn—and I liked having the sound inside the trailer with me. Outside, the street was quiet. The lights were low at the minimart. I hoped Soula was sleeping.

In my bunk, I opened my writer's notebook and took a look at the "Sloppy Copy" of my school essay. *Sloppy* barely described it. My writing was okay. But I had things crossed out, eraser marks everywhere, and worst of all, I'd missed the left margin for most of the new lines—again. My work covered only the right half of the page and it was on a slant. Like a quilting square cut on a diagonal.

Why was it so hard? My teacher and I had gone through my entire writer's notebook and had highlighted every left-hand margin in bright pink. When I wrote, I was supposed to come back and bump that pink edge with the first letter of every new line. It seemed like kindergarten stuff. But if I got my mind going on the words, I started to miss the margin. If I concentrated on the margin, I forgot what I was writing.

I sighed loudly, and Piccolo's wheel stopped. She was looking at me. "I can't do it, Pic," I said. I rolled onto my back and covered my face with the open notebook. "Grrrrr . . . How do ya get the Love of Learning?"

Helena and Marissa had been nice to me about all my school stuff. That was a relief. I never looked forward to explaining my learning problems to a new classroom full of kids.

"Is this part so you can make notes and corrections?" Marissa had asked. She'd patted the blank wedge of space in my notebook with her open hand.

I was tempted to say yes. I rolled my eyes. "No, I just have some kind of *spatial relationship* problems.

That's what the special education teacher told me. It happens in reading, too," I said. "Words sort of slide on the page." I swept my hand to one side.

When my teacher had given me a laminated strip of oaktag to use for reading, Helena asked for one too.

"It really helps," she'd said. The two of us had sat shoulder to shoulder in the classroom reading nook together, moving our oaktag strips down the pages of our books.

Now I listened to a freight train go by on the tracks above and behind me and wondered for a moment what it was carrying and where it was going. That made me think of Mommers again. I wondered what she would be selling in her new business. Was it something the trains would bring? Would it go right by our trailer before it reached the store or the warehouse or whatever? And, the big question: Would it really work out?

I watched Piccolo disappear into her tissue nest for a nap. The trailer was quiet. Too quiet. I checked the time again. Five past twelve. I thought about my wish.

"Come back, Mommers," I whispered. I started to feel scared. But not from being alone—that never really bothered me so much. It was the kind of scared you get from a memory. When something begins to feel like another time—a time when things didn't go right. A time we took some twists and turns. It was late; that was part of it. Mommers had stayed out late like this before. Then she stayed later and later, and after that, she'd stopped coming home.

I remembered the waiting. I was nine, Brynna was three and Katie was a year old. The divorce had already happened and Dwight lived nearby in an apartment but he was on a job in Vermont for the week. He'd called to talk to us every night—not to Mommers. Just to us.

Brynna, Katie and I had all been in the big bed together at the old house. They lay asleep. I lay awake.

Mommers had called the first two nights. "Addie, my business plan is going really well. It's just gonna take a little more time."

"Can't you work on the plan here?"

"I'll be back soon enough, and you're there for the babies. See, I planned this for your winter vacation week. You're fine, aren't you," she'd said. But it didn't sound like a question and she didn't wait for an answer. "I'll call tomorrow night," she'd said. Click.

But she didn't call. Dwight did, and for some reason he asked for Mommers. I stayed quiet on the line. I watched the snow coming down outside on the deck where I'd left the light on for her.

"Addie, is she home?"

I had to whisper back to him. "No," I said.

"What?"

"Not here," I said.

"How long has she been gone?" he asked.

I said, "Three."

"Days?"

"Yes."

"Oh God." His voice went down like my own sinking heart. "Are the babies okay?"

"Sleeping," I whispered. "I'm home from school this week, Dwight. We're okay."

"Is there food?"

"Peanut butter jellies."

"You warm? Furnace running?"

I listened for the hum. "Yes."

"Door locked, honey?"

"Yes."

"Addie, I'm calling Grandio. He can get there

quickly. And I'm getting in the truck right now. I'll see you in a couple of hours. Depends on the snow, but I'm coming home."

I put the phone on the cradle. I knew everything was ruined.

When Grandio got to us that night, he came pushing through the door as soon as I unlocked it. I had to hop back so the door wouldn't scrape the tops of my toes.

"This is what I always said. That woman leaves a whole lotta nothin' good every place she goes!" He ran his hand through his gray hairs. "Doesn't she know she's left her own *babies* home alone?" He searched the messy house for a fresh diaper for Katie even though I told him over and over again that it was better to just let her sleep. "Who knows when the last time was that kid got a clean bottom!" he raged. "The mother's been gone for three days!"

"I changed Katie before bed, Grandio. Let her sleep. She'll just be scared," I pleaded.

Finally, he listened to me about the diaper. But he also said, "This is it. This is *child abandonment*. This is all we need. It's over."

late-night mail

"Psst! Addie!"

"What?" I opened my eyes. I sat up in the dark and looked at Mommers. "You're back! What time is it?"

"Dunno. Two, I guess. I just wanted you to know I'm here."

"Late," I said. I heard the computer booting up. "What are you doing?"

"Checking my e-mail. And I gotta shoot a note to Pete, too."

"Pete?"

"That's who I had dinner with. We worked on the business plan. Oh, Addie, he's so smart!" she said. "And gorgeous, too."

"Plan? I thought it was an interview."

75

"Go back to sleep." Mommers sat down and started typing.

I lay back in my bunk but I couldn't go back to sleep. I heard Mommers go into the bathroom. I climbed down from my bunk and I looked at the computer screen, where an unsent e-mail glowed back.

> Pete:
> Loved our meeting. This is going to be great! Will see about finding more investors. Hope my contribution helps. See you online.
>
> Denise

Mommers came out of the bathroom and I faced her squarely.

"Did you give him our money from Dwight?"

She put her hands on her hips and gave me a frown.

another dish of fish-and-chips

I never got a straight answer out of Mommers that night. She didn't say she had given *Pete* our money but she didn't say she hadn't either. For weeks she kept on meeting him, sometimes late into the night, and she spent a lot of time on the computer. Our phone line was almost never open. Even though she'd said something about *her contribution* in that e-mail message, we didn't seem to be having money troubles. Mommers had new "business clothes," which she wore on her late-night meetings with Pete. The trailer was filling up with office supplies. She even bought Halloween decorations that looked like coloring book drawings and she put them up all over the trailer. We had ghosts in top hats and flying bats on the walls.

She put a pumpkin face over the bare light bulb in the kitchen. In the meantime, we were out of bread.

Ms. Rivera came to my classroom to get me. She invited me into the hallway. "Addie, you've earned a spot in the Stage Orchestra." She smiled.

I leaped inside of my own skin.

"I've been trying to call your home but the line has been busy."

"My mother uses the Internet a lot," I said, "for work."

"Well, here's a note you can give her. Practices are *mandatory*." She tilted her head at me. "Monday and Thursday after school. We rest during Thanksgiving break. You'll need an outfit. Black on the bottom, white on the top. Your choice, but simple works best. The holiday concert is always the second Friday in December." She took a breath. "I think that's it. Are you happy?"

"Yes! Thank you."

I rushed back inside the classroom to tell Helena and Marissa. "Makes me wish I was in orchestra," Marissa said. "But I'll be in the audience."

"The audience is important!" Helena said, and

we laughed because it was so true.

Robert overheard us and he actually smiled. "That's good you made it."

I squinted at him. "Why are you being nice?"

He shrugged. "Think you can keep up learning the new music?"

Everyone in my class knew that I was a mess when it came to learning anything new.

I took a breath. "Yes," I said. "I know I can."

Mommers got very excited about my spot in Stage Orchestra. She pinned the letter to the fridge and circled the concert date on the kitchen calendar with a sparkle pen from her office supplies.

"Let's celebrate!" she said. "Let's go out to eat. How about Numbskull Dorry's? Within walking distance!" she sang.

"Can we afford it?"

She waved a shiny credit card at me and danced a cha-cha.

I stopped in my happy-tracks. "Whose is that?" I asked.

"Mine!" she said. "I got it from Pete. It's for the business, but I can pay on it. Come on, Addie! Let's have some fun!" She leaned right into my face and said, "Can you say that? *Fun*?" She scowled at me, then grinned. "Lighten up, kid! I'm employed!"

We had a blast. First we dressed up more than we needed to. Mommers tossed me some of her clothes to try, which didn't quite fit. I felt funny in lady clothes but Mommers talked me into wearing one of the shirts. She borrowed a glow-in-the-dark necklace from me and we both painted our fingernails—Mommers in hot orange, me with the clear stuff. We put our hair up on top of our heads and used rhinestone bobby pins to hold back the wisps.

At Numbskull Dorry's, I ordered first.

"Fish-and-chips, please," I said.

"Fish-and-chips," Mommers teased. "How predictable!"

But I surprised her when I asked the waitress, "Is Rick in the kitchen tonight?"

"You bet. Who shall I say is here?" the waitress asked.

"Addie," I said. "From the minimart."

"Well, it's busy, but if he can get a second, I'm sure he'll come out." The waitress hurried off.

Mommers pretended to be French, and she was loud about it, too. "Oddie from zee minimart?" She let her voice rise and fall. "And who is zee gentleman, *Reek?*" The people from the next booth looked over at us and smiled at our fun. I felt my cheeks turn warm.

"Not Reek! *Rick!*" I whispered. "He's just the *owner*." I tried to keep a straight face but I was no good at that.

Mommers sat back, her hand to her heart. "You've been keeping secrets! My, my, Oddie dahling! Tell me more!"

I leaned forward and said, "When you call me Oddie, you sound like Katie!" We burst out laughing. Maybe it was just something about Numbskull Dorry's. It was a good-times place for us.

Rick came out while we were having dessert. He greeted us as if we were his most important friends. He sat right down and Mommers flirted with him. I didn't bother to tell her that he had a boyfriend.

Later we walked home in the cool October night. The streetlamps lit the city sidewalks and jack-o'-lantern faces glowed from the porches and windows of the houses on Union Street. Halloween was just a few days off. I was sorry I would not be trick-or-treating with my little sisters. I wondered if my old Dalmatian costume had fit Brynna, and if Katie had found something that would make her into a hamster—she wanted to be Piccolo, she'd told me.

Mommers put her hand on my shoulder to slow me in front of a brick house on a corner lot. Two orange pumpkins grinned in shining slices from a bench by the door. Little tissue ghosts hung from the knobby branches of a small tree beside the gate.

Mommers bit her bottom lip and narrowed her eyes. "We're gonna get a new place soon, Addison," she told me. "Maybe even by Christmas."

I was not focused on Christmas at all. I was focused on the second Friday in December, which happened to be the twelfth. That was the night of our Stage Orchestra performance.

I worked on the music every night and tried to be ready for each practice. Ms. Rivera kept her arrangement with me and I got the score ahead of everyone else so I could start "assimilating" it. I looked up *assimilate*. Webster's listed some scientific terms like *digest* and *metabolize* first. But the second definition seemed closer to me. It said, "to absorb and incorporate, as in knowledge." But to me, the word that made the most sense was *learn*: "to master through study."

Bingo!

a different sort
of halloween

I guess you could say that Halloween came and went that year, or should have. Like I say, I was pretty focused on December 12, but I did try and get Marissa and Helena to go trick-or-treating with me. I thought we could start at Helena's, hit Seneca, and then cross to Union and come down the other side. That would have been about thirty houses—pretty good loot. But Helena's mom took her kids to a neighborhood across the bridge, which was safer, she said, and it turned out that Marissa's parents didn't allow her to trick-or-treat at all.

So I changed my plan. I'd do just Union and have Mommers walk out on the street with me. "We can look at the houses again," I told her.

But Mommers put it to me bluntly. "Addie, Halloween is for little kids. Maybe some of the kids in your class are still little but *you* aren't."

"Helena is *taller* than I am. She's going."

Mommers sighed through her teeth. "You're short, but, Addie, you have *boobs*, in case you hadn't noticed. People will turn you away."

"Helena's boobs are bigger," I mumbled.

"Besides, I have plans," Mommers told me.

Soula and Elliot felt bad for me when I walked into the minimart after school and told them I had nothing to do on Halloween night.

"Oh, come over *here*!" Elliot said, arms open. "You can dress up! I always do. You can hand out candy at the counter."

I grinned. I didn't have a costume but one walk through Soula's closet fixed that. Elliot put one of her big dresses on me—dropped it right over my own clothes—and belted it around me with two scarves. He helped me paint my face at Soula's vanity table. He lined my eyes and drew in pointed lashes that came halfway down my cheeks. He gave me a big, bright, Soula-pink mouth, and finished me off with a straw hat covered in purple fake flowers. "You're a She-clown!" he said. He gave the hat a pat.

"Tah-dah!" Elliot announced me as we came back into the minimart from the Greenhouse.

"I don't get it," Soula said. She looked from me to Elliot and back at me again. "Where's her costume?"

Silence. I looked at Elliot. He was turning red right up the neck.

Soula pointed a finger at him. "Gotcha!" she wailed. She burst out laughing, head back, pink mouth wide open.

"Oh, you are *terrible*!" Elliot said, swatting at her. She slapped back, still giggling.

"Hey, Little Cookie? You didn't let him shave your head too, did you?"

"Oh, Soula!" I gulped. Then I laughed.

"Oh, now that's *really* bad." Elliot shook his head and raised one hand in the air to make her stop.

Soula turned to me and sighed. "Ha-ha! I got him good, didn't I?" I met her hands in a double high-five and we laced our fingers together.

"You got me too," I said, and we held on to each other for a moment longer.

· · ·

I held Soula's big dress up around my knees and started home to tell Mommers where I'd be that night. As I crossed the street, I could see Mr. and Mrs. Rose inside the Heads and Roses Laundry Stop. The mannequin heads in the front window were all decked out in black and orange with witches' hats and spidery wigs and the Roses were placing jack-o'-lanterns between them. When they saw me they started laughing and that made me laugh. I must have been quite a sight. I waved back with big sweeps of my arm.

I was dying to have Mommers see my costume, but when I opened the trailer door I could tell something was wrong.

One cigarette burned in the ashtray by the computer. Mommers held a second one in her lips. She was clawing through the boxes of new office supplies. She brought out two packages of Bic pens, a handful of Wite-Outs and a box of binder clips, and dumped them on the table.

"Hi," I said.

She slammed two plastic file boxes into each other and swore. She pushed her fingers into her hair, let a breath out and finally looked at me and her cigarette bobbed up and down.

"Are you looking for something?" I asked.

"Oh God. Look at you." She rolled her eyes at me.

I had forgotten about my made-up face. "Oh yeah." I grinned. "I'm gonna hand out candy at the minimart tonight."

Mommers shook her head. "I told you you're too old for that stuff."

"I'm not trick-or-treating. Besides, even Elliot dresses up."

"You just can't do it the way *I* say, can you, Addison?" She sighed.

"I don't want to miss out on Halloween," I said.

"Well, I'm going out," Mommers said.

"To work?"

"Yes. I'm meeting Pete."

"Mommers, when is all this stuff going to the office?" I asked.

"This *is* the office. The office is at *my* house."

"House?" I felt a twinge of sickness inside of me. Mommers was telling lies to Pete.

"When everything gets up and running, we *will* have a house, and then I'll tell Pete about how little we actually started with. And I'll tell him about you and—"

"He doesn't know you have a kid? *Three* kids."

"What he doesn't know won't hurt him," she insisted.

I looked at all the office supplies. "When are you going to set it all up? When do you start using the stuff?"

Mommers looked at the boxes all around her. She took a fast hard drag on her cigarette and blew the smoke back out. "You think I bought too much, don't you? You know what, Addie? You have to spend money to make money. It's in every business text and journal across the country. Why . . . why are you asking me this anyway?" She shook her hair back.

"I just wondered," I said.

Mommers went into her bedroom and when she came out she flung a small overnight bag onto the table. She disappeared again, into the bathroom this time, and came out with fresh makeup, her hair sprayed up, and new earrings on.

"Pete and I are taking a short business trip," she said. "A little overnighter. It won't be a big deal and you can take care of yourself."

"A trip? But, Mommers . . ."

"Oh, Addie, don't! Please! Just don't! I can't

take it. I'm trying to put together a life here!" She shook her head and put her hands up like she was trying to stop something in the air.

I watched her just a second. I knew that she needed me to say it was okay, but I couldn't do that any more than I could keep her from going. Mommers was like that. If she decided something needed buying, she bought it. If she decided to go out all night, she went.

"Is there bread?" I asked.

Mommers huffed and opened her purse. She took out a ten-dollar bill and slapped it on the counter. "There," she said. She stopped to breathe. "Buy bread from your friends." She motioned toward the minimart.

I followed her out and watched her marching up the street toward the bus station on her business heels.

I fed Piccolo a little carrot tip—I ate the rest. I slogged back over to the minimart—not because I wanted to anymore, just because there was nothing else to do. It turned out the place was quiet. I guess everyone got their treats and gasoline before the big night so they wouldn't need to make a stop right in the middle of it. We saw half a dozen customers and I gave candy bars to five of them. The sixth one was a diabetic; he told me.

Soula and Elliot tried to entertain me by putting candy corns and pumpkin-shaped marshmallows into the microwave and turning it on high. That was kind of funny the first time and I liked listening to Soula laugh so hard. But it got messy and soon I felt bored with the game. They tuned the store TV in to one of those Fright Night shows. Soula sat in her lawn chair and Elliot hopped up on the checkout counter to watch. I pulled up a milk crate but I didn't last long.

Around eight thirty, I told them I was going to wander home. It's hard to *wander* when you only live fifty feet away. I stopped out by the island where the customers pump their gas and wrapped my hand around the pole that held up the rain roof there. I let my weight take me around and around in low swinging dips, my hand squeaking along the column. Each time the Heads and Roses Laundry Stop went by I caught the glowing jack-o'-lanterns in my sight line. I should do our laundry, I thought. I kept going around and around until I could feel heat and a blister coming up in my palm.

I crossed the street, walked back to the rope swing Dwight had put up and turned myself as much upside down on it as I could. Soula's scarves hung down from my waist and brushed the bottom of my chin. As the swing moved back and forth it whined and I could see first the night sky, then the darkness of the Over-Underpass.

When my head got stuffy from being upside down, I sat plain on the swing and toed the busted pavement until I loosened a chunk. I kicked it away. My nose cleared. A fumy sort of stink was in the air. It might have been exhaust. It might have been something I'd put my hand in back at the pump.

I sniffed. So this is the smell and the feel of Halloween this year, I told myself. No sweets. No trick-or-treating. No candy bars to sort and trade. No fun. No Dwight, no Brynna, no Katie. I looked at the dark trailer. No Mommers.

a phone call from the mansion

Halloween was on a Friday night. By Saturday afternoon I had begun to watch for Mommers—*really* watch. The suitcase she'd taken was small.

"She has to come back," I told Piccolo. My hamster looked up from her belly washing, twitched her whiskers at me and went back to her work. I pressed my nose against the front window and looked up Nott Street thinking I'd see Mommers coming down the hill from the bus stop. The phone rang.

Mommers?

I stumbled over the file boxes to answer it. "Hello?"

"Addie? That you?"

"Dwight! Yes! Hi!" I tucked the phone closer to my ear.

"Did you have a good Halloween?"

"Great," I lied. "Did you?"

"Pretty good. Missed you though. We got some pictures, honey. The Littles want you to see their costumes."

"Tell them I can't wait," I said.

"Tell 'em yourself." Dwight was smiling when he said that. I knew without even seeing him.

"Oddie, Oddie!" Katie squealed. "I was a hampister for Holloween! Honnah made me ears. She putted them on a headbond."

Then I heard Brynna laugh. I was surprised. She seemed to be on her own receiver. "Head*band*!" she said. "She put the ears on a head*band*!"

"Who's Honnah?" I asked.

"She means *Hannah*." Brynna giggled.

"Honnah lives all to home at the big, big house."

"What?"

"She means at the mansion," Brynna said.

When they gave me back to Dwight, I said, "Did you get another phone?"

"Well sort of. Listen, we moved. Still in Lake George. Better and cheaper. I got a new number for ya. Take this down, okay?" I wrote, then he asked me to repeat it back, which I did.

"Perfect," he said.

"Dwight?"

"Yeah?"

"Who's *Honnah*, or *Hannah*?"

"Ahh, Hannah. Well . . . I want you to meet her," he said, and right away I knew Dwight felt something special for her. "In fact, I'm trying to set something up. I can't get down there until Thanksgiving, Addie."

"Thanksgiving? That's *three* weeks away," I groaned, and then felt bad.

"I know, I know. But let me see what I can do here." Then he asked, "Is your mom home?"

"Uh . . . not right now. She'll be back soon though."

He paused. "Okay. Well, this is what I'm shooting for. You can give her the message. I'm coming to Grandio's for Thanksgiving. That's a Thursday."

"Uh-huh."

"Okay. And then, I'd like to bring you back here with me after that."

"All right!"

"Think you can spend the night? Maybe Friday

and Saturday too? I could put you on the bus Sunday morning if you're cool with that."

I thought I was going to pee my pants. "Yes!" I squealed into the phone. "I can take the bus alone. I can come!" I said.

"We gotta check everything with Denise, Addie."

"I know."

"Okay, kiddo. How is your mom anyway?"

"Great! She's real busy. She has an office," I said. I looked at the empty plastic file boxes near my feet and shut my eyes for a second.

"That's good to hear," Dwight said.

"Yep. She's doing great," I repeated.

"I'll check back with you about Thanksgiving, then. Love you."

"Love you, too."

We said good-bye.

I grabbed a paper shopping bag, boxed it open and packed for the trip. I didn't care that it was still three weeks away. I wanted to be ready.

Saturday turned into Sunday and Mommers still didn't show. But I was okay. I still had bread in the trailer, and change from the ten if I needed anything else. And *now* I had something to look forward to.

the new blue car

On Monday morning I ate my toast. I stepped out of the trailer still pulling on my backpack and bumping myself with my flute case as I went.

Beep! Beep!

A car horn scared me back a few steps. I looked and there was Mommers in the driver's seat. She pulled onto the tar patch out front and stopped hard.

"Surprise!" she screamed from the open window.

I grabbed my heart with one hand and steadied myself.

"Get in! Get in! I'll drive you to school!"

The car just happened to be my favorite shade of blue.

"Addie! Come on!" Mommers got out. She ran

around the car, hugged me and sang out, "'Baby, you can drive my car . . .'" from some old song I barely recognized. She swung me left, then right, the weight of my pack nearly dumping me over.

"Watch out for the flute," I said. I held the instrument case up and away from her. She yanked the car door open and pushed me inside.

"This looks like a kidnapping, ya know."

Mommers went into a huge laughing fit over that. She slammed my door shut and shimmied along the bumper to the driver's side. She landed hard on the seat, then lay on the horn a few times for fun. "Don't ya love it? Hot, hot, hot!" I rolled my window up as fast as I could. She let out a few choice swears and hit the horn again.

I caught sight of Soula at that moment. She was standing out in front of the minimart—probably wondering what all the commotion was about.

Mommers giggled and waved at Soula. "Oooh! Look who's watching us! Woo-hoo! Bye-bye, *big* girl!"

I faked backpack problems so I wouldn't have to look at Soula. I was pretty sure she hadn't heard what Mommers had said. Mommers beeped the horn again and I frowned at her. She pouted back but not for real. She stepped on the gas and we were off with a screech.

The car smelled great, like new rugs and plastic. Of course, it wasn't really new but I thought almost any car smelled great. I couldn't even remember my last car ride—probably with Grandio months ago. The upholstery felt velvety good under my palm now, and the ride was easy over the potholes on Nott Street. We zipped past Hose Company No. 6.

"Are you gonna ask me?" Mommers finally said. She wiggled in her seat.

"Ask what? Where you've been?" I raised an eyebrow.

"About the car," she rattled back at me.

I shook my head. "Nope."

"Well gee, thanks for the support, Addison," Mommers said.

I got out of the car at school and she stuck her head out of the window. "You're as much fun as bird poop on a windshield, ya know."

I shrugged. Maybe she was right.

all or nothing

"Hey, Little Cookie? Where you been?" Soula tucked one finger up under her wig for a scratch.

"Oh, around," I said. I knew she meant that she hadn't seen me over the weekend. I'd stayed inside the trailer feeling like it was my job to be there— like I had to hold down the fort until Mommers got back.

"Everything okay over at your place?" Soula poked her chin in the direction of the trailer.

"Yeah," I said. I tried to sound natural, even perky. I took the broom out of the corner by the checkout and started sweeping the floor.

"Hey, Cookie . . ." Soula hesitated.

"What?" I stopped working to look at her.

"Does your mama have some troubles?"

I didn't answer.

"Maybe something with her moods?" Soula said. "Does she get real happy, then real sad? I mean more so than other people you know?"

I twisted the broom in my hands. I shrugged. "I don't know," I said.

I knew that if I told anyone Mommers had been gone all those days, it'd be the same as last time: something bad would happen because of it.

"She's got a new job," I blurted. "Been working real hard at it, too. She's kind of an all-or-nothing person, I guess."

I left the minimart right after that. I went home thinking, All or nothing, all or nothing. I realized how true that was.

Mommers was always getting ideas. Big ideas. She always dove right in, too, like she was in a hurry, like a person trying to catch up. She didn't go to college when she finished high school. She was having me instead. She always said she hadn't gotten to fulfill her Love of Learning.

But Mommers had kept trying. One of her ideas had been about going to school to become a nurse. That was right after Brynna was born. Dwight wanted Mommers to go and he said they'd find a way to pay for it. He changed his hours at work so he could be home with Brynna and me while Mommers went to class. She started night school. She came home with all the textbooks and sat on the bed with them opened so I could look with her. I watched her label all her new notebooks with perfect, straight letters for each subject.

"I love medicine," she'd told me. She'd snapped the cap back on her pen. "Do you know that the best time of my life was being in the hospital having you? And then again with Brynna? Birth is so exciting, Addie! If I could put that experience in a package and sell it, I'd be rich. Everybody would want it. I'm going to be a great labor-and-delivery nurse."

But something happened to the nursing school idea. She stopped going just like that. It was so hard to understand because it had been her *all*. Then suddenly, it was *nothing*.

Then, after Katie was born, Mommers got a new idea. She decided to become a psychologist and help people with their problems. Again she came home with all the books and her class schedule. Dwight bought her a computer to do her work on. But soon she said she needed to do her studying at the library. She was gone every night. She slept late every morning.

One night, Grandio came to take care of Brynna and Katie and me. Dwight went out and when he came home he brought Mommers with him. She kicked and screamed and cried for hours. She stayed in bed the next day—doing nothing. Dwight took on more jobs. He was working from sunup to sundown—sometimes longer. That's when I started making toast dinners.

When Mommers finally got up, she discovered the Internet. She started chatting with all sorts of people who had great business ideas. She stayed online through the day and into the night. That became her *all*. But Dwight didn't like that. I'd hear them arguing—something about losing money on the Internet. There was a lot of fighting until finally Mommers said she wanted the divorce. Dwight moved out and some time after that Mommers packed a bag and left us alone for those three nights in the middle of winter.

That was the time I blew it—the time I told Dwight that she was gone. That split us all up, pretty much for good.

dwight explaining hannah

It turned out that it was fine with Mommers for me to go to Grandio's for Thanksgiving supper and on to Lake George with Dwight afterward.

"If you really want to go to Jack's farm for Turkey Day, okay. But there's no way I'm going," she said. She was watching *Jeanette for the Judgment* and didn't take her eyes off the show. "*Stick it to him, Jeanette!*" she cheered. "Jack will be just as glad if I'm not there. I'll make my own plans. *Judgment for the defense!* I'm gonna do something with Pete. And if Dwight wants you for a couple of nights, that's cool with me. *Make him pay her back!* I have plenty to do. Just get on the right bus back here come Sunday, will ya?" Then she mumbled, "I can just see myself driving up and down the Northway . . ."

"I'll get the bus," I said.

She dropped me and my paper bag suitcase and my flute (had to practice) off at Grandio's farm on Thanksgiving Day. "Don't forget to feed Piccolo," I reminded her. She waved a hand at me and sped away. I watched her blue car rolling and bumping away down Grandio's rough driveway. The hillside was covered in that long yellow November grass that looks like it's been combed into low humps. The trees in the orchard were bare except for a few dry old apples still clinging here and there. The sour smell of fallen fruit still hung in the air. I spun around slowly, letting my flute case and my paper bag fly along beside me in my outstretched arms. I remembered climbing in those apple branches with the Littles while Dwight and Grandio worked on the old barn together, while they mowed the fields, while they raked leaves. I remembered Grandio saying that having Dwight around was like having a son again. I remembered family birthday parties, sit-down suppers and everyone together under one roof. I remembered us just being *normal*.

It's good to be here again—good to be across the bridge, I thought, as I made myself dizzy. For a second, I forgot where I lived, which place was home.

"Addie? Jeepers, girl! Git in here!"

I stopped twirling, but the world did not. "Hi, Grandio," I called. I staggered forward a few steps, then waited. When everything had stopped spinning, I smiled to see him standing in his apron at the door to the stone farmhouse. He was squinting at me like I was nuts. I ran a few steps so as not to keep him waiting.

The good smells from the kitchen hit me at the door. Grandio had done Thanksgiving like I'd never seen it done before. He had stuffed and roasted a turkey and had made brown gravy. There were whipped potatoes keeping on the stovetop, green beans in the steamer, cranberry-orange sauce in little china dishes on the table and baskets of bread on the sideboard.

"How's everything with you, girl?" he asked. But I already knew that Grandio didn't listen for answers much.

"Place looks great," I said. It was true. A fire roared in the fireplace, there was bittersweet on the mantel. The candles waited to be lit. He lifted an apple salad out of the fridge and added it to the spread.

"You've thought of everything!" I said. And

soon I knew the reason why.

Dwight and the Littles arrived about a minute later. With them they brought three different kinds of pie and another person—a pretty woman in a long skirt and a big sweater. She threw a thick brown braid over her shoulder and waved a mitten-covered hand at Grandio and me as she strode toward us.

Hannah.

In a second, Brynna and Katie were all over me, both talking at once and giggling about a turkey song they'd learned. Everything was hugs and greetings and the swish of jackets being run up the stairs to Grandio's spare bedroom.

"Where's Mommers?" Brynna asked suddenly. Katie stopped still and looked around the bedroom almost like she wasn't sure who we were talking about.

"She couldn't come," I said, knowing it was more like *wouldn't*. I glanced at Hannah and figured that was just as well. "She's having turkey dinner with Pete. She works with him."

"Work? Humph," said Grandio. He wrestled a jacket onto a hanger. "That woman wouldn't know *work* if it walked up and punched her in the nose." I frowned at him but he didn't see me. "And she goes through men like corn through a hen. And the results are about the same."

That wasn't the first time I'd heard him say that.

Dwight put his hand up. "Jack," he said softly, and that was all.

I didn't see why Grandio had to put Mommers down—again—especially with this new Hannah person watching. Hannah shifted her stance and looked at Dwight. "Well, gee, the whole house smells so good!" she said. She rubbed her hands together. She had a smile that came easily and took up most of her face. She looked at Grandio and he seemed to soften as he grinned back at her.

"I better get back to the kitchen. Turkey isn't gonna baste itself," Grandio said. He hurried toward the stairs.

"We'll be right down," Dwight called after him.

Hannah turned to me. "Addie, I feel like I know you." She had a voice like butter and brown sugar. "Do you know how often we talk about you at home?"

That was kind of weird. They all had a home that I wasn't part of. I looked Hannah over. I'd known all of them longer than she had. Those were *my* baby sisters and Dwight had been my step-father longer than she'd known him. Something inside me wanted to tell her so. But I kept turning soft. I liked her wide smile. It was real.

Dwight put his hand on the back of my neck and gave me a squeeze. "Can't wait to get you up to Lake George," he said. I leaned into him, then felt the warm pop of his lips kissing my head.

"We should warn you, Addie, the place is kinda a mess," Hannah said. She tilted her head at Dwight and they both laughed.

"Yeah, I should really explain . . . um . . . every-thing." Dwight shuffled his feet. Hannah cleared her throat.

"I'll leave you two to catch up," she said. "See you both downstairs." She brushed Dwight's arm with her hand and herded my sisters into the hall. "Let's let Dwight talk to Addie. Shall we go see your granddad's fire, girls? Hmm? Let's go warm our hands."

"They're cold and wosy," Katie said. I could hear her feet as she two-stepped her way down the stairs.

"She means *rosy*," Brynna added, her voice fad-ing.

The upstairs was quiet.

"So what's going on?" I asked Dwight.

He blinked. "Boy, you sound so much older the way you just said that."

I shrugged. No matter what else he had to tell me, at least I wouldn't hear anything about boobs from Dwight.

"Um, listen. Hannah and I are . . . well, we're . . . uh . . ."

"You like her," I helped.

"Oh yeah." He grinned. Then he got serious. "I never expected this. Not now. She was just my boss, ya know?"

"Boss? At work? Hannah owns that mansion you're working on?"

"Yeah. She's turning it into an inn—a bed-and-breakfast. She has investors but it's her place. She makes all the decisions. And, man, I've never seen anybody work harder."

"She sounds awesome," I whispered, and Dwight nodded.

"This whole thing has been such a surprise, Addie. It's been fast." He ran his hand through his hair. "I just meant to stay focused and do the work. Pay off the debts. But then . . . Hannah and I started spending time together and she does so much for the Littles. And it all comes so easily somehow . . ."

I swallowed. "I've found some friends too," I said. I thought of Soula and Elliot, and Helena and Marissa. "So, I know what you mean. It feels good to care about someone else," I said.

"Exactly." He let a second go by. "And this is serious. We'd like to get married this summer, Addie."

"Oh," I said. A funny little breath went through my lips. "Things must be *really* good."

"Great! Things are great."

"And you moved?" I said.

"Yes." He shuffled his feet again. "We live with Hannah. We're making one section of the inn into our home. It's not finished, but it's warm, dry and comfortable. It's better for the Littles this way. It really is. One of us is always there for them." He paused. "And Hannah loves them both."

I nodded. "They are really great, aren't they? I mean they are easy to love, and Hannah seems so nice. Looks like they like her, too."

"I think so," Dwight said. "I wish it could be all of us, you know that?"

I couldn't answer him then. I was thinking of the way Katie always said ". . . all to home." I swallowed against a lump in my throat and gave Dwight a little punch in the shoulder. I stopped him on the stairs a minute later and told him, "Thanks for telling me everything."

all about twos and fours

Late that afternoon Hannah and I sat on a pair of footstools by Grandio's fading fire, just the two of us. This was not by mistake; I had wanted to get her alone. Flames still wrapped the sides of a slender log or two but most of the fire had settled down to coals.

"I love the embers," Hannah said with a Thanksgiving sort of sigh.

"Me too," I said. I watched them winking red and orange a few seconds longer. But I needed to get to my business—the business of being nosy with Hannah. This was more than a get-to-know-your-neighbors mission. Hannah was with my little sisters all the time—beneath the same roof. She was with them as much as a mother would be with her children, I thought. Dwight trusted her, so I did too—mostly—but I still wanted to know more about her.

"Hey, Hannah," I said, "I was wondering something. What did you do before you got the inn?"

"Well, there's a good question," Hannah said. She sat up a bit. "I like to say that my adult life has been all about twos and fours." She showed me two fingers, then four fingers, then two again. She pushed her hands forward when she did this almost like she was dancing from her little seat by the fire.

"Twos and fours?" I closed one eye at her and she laughed.

"That's right." Hannah kept her fingers switching from two to four and back and told me, "When I was eighteen I graduated from high school. Then I waited tables for *two* years. Then I went to college for *four* years. After that I planned a cross-country trip with *two* friends. That trip was supposed to last *four* weeks, but I liked the West so much I got a job and stayed for *two* years." She stopped, took a breath and planted her hands on her knees. "Then both my parents got sick. I came back east to be with them. They passed on within *four* months of each other."

"Oh, how sad!" I said. "I mean, I know you can't help it if that's part of the story and all. But it's so . . ."

"Sad. You're right," said Hannah. "But oddly enough there were good things about it too. We got to be together all those days. I loved taking care of them, really, and dear friends visited every day." She waited, then leaned forward as if she were about to tell a secret. She brought her hands together under her chin. "Then . . . *two* days before I was all set to go back west again, I saw the inn in the real estate pages. Just by chance. Suddenly, I loved the idea of a home—a big home with lots of rooms!" Hannah flung her arms wide open. "I wanted lots of people to be coming and going. I wanted to cook big breakfasts every morning and hang sheets to dry in the mountain air!" Hannah laughed at herself for that last part. "So, I asked for a showing of the inn, and the agent gave me lots of time to wander around inside. It'd been years since anyone had operated it as a business, and oh, room after room, it was a mess. Worse than what you'll see when you get there, Addie!" Hannah scrunched her nose and laughed. "But I could imagine it all redone." She closed her eyes for a second. "I was so charmed by the idea of bringing the place back to life that I took a big chance. I used all the money my mom and dad had left me to make the down payment. Of course, now I've borrowed a lot, too. So I have a small business that I run from the inn—you'll see that, too. Everything seems to be falling into place. I still get nervous." Hannah shook her whole body and laughed. "I've never been much of a planner—can you tell? But now . . . well, Dwight and you three girls have given me . . . ha!"—she showed me four fingers—"*four* good reasons to plan." She stretched her legs out in a satisfied way. "I never expected all of you to come into my life." Hannah wore a puzzled grin. "Yet here we are. Instant family," she said.

I had never had a more thankful Thanksgiving Day. I felt pretty sure that my little sisters had themselves a new hero.

bedtime at the inn

We arrived in Lake George under the bright moonlight of Thanksgiving night. We had traveled a winding mountain road up to the inn. Brynna slumped against me, asleep, on the back-seat of the car. Katie was out cold in her car seat on my other side. I craned to see the mansion. My paper bag suitcase crackled between my feet each time I moved.

"This is the place," Dwight whispered. He turned back from the front seat to look at me through the darkness. The building was big. I'd expected that. But it was also prettier than I'd imag-ined, like a real house for lots of people to stay in. I got the sense of lots of little peaks in the roof and there was a long porch and double-door entrance at the center. Ladders and scaffolding leaned up against the front, waiting for the workers.

"You must love it here," I whispered back. "I can't wait to see it in daylight."

I wanted to carry Katie inside but Hannah got to her first, me being wedged in the middle like I was. She gently lifted the buckle of the car seat over my little sister's fuzzy head. She bent to pick up Katie, draping the little hands around her neck before she rose. She knows just what to do, I thought. Dwight woke Brynna and hoisted her onto his hip. I carried my bag and the flute.

We climbed a small side porch and entered a little hall where Dwight's tool belt hung on a nail. We stepped over Katie's yellow duck boots and Brynna's green frog ones. I followed Dwight and Hannah through the unfinished kitchen. There were no cabinets. The cans and boxes of food sat on open shelves. Beyond that was a room with a window that bumped out so you could sit in it. There was a couch, a chair and a TV set, and my sisters' toys in a big basket in one corner. I smelled new wood all around me. Wall studs showed through plastic sheeting in some places. Little piles of wood shavings needed sweeping.

"Told you it was a mess," Hannah said. She

grinned. "We're kind of camped out right now, but it'll get better. We'll show you around tomorrow."

I nodded and followed her to the door of a bedroom, where she knelt to ease Katie onto a junior bed. Across the room, Dwight sat Brynna on the bottom of a bunk bed and pulled off her shoes.

"Top's for you," he said, raising his chin at me.

I nodded again.

He squinted at me. "Addie, you okay?" Hannah had turned to look at me too. I just stood still. Truth was I didn't know what was wrong. It was *only* bedtime—happens every night. But it was strange to watch them doing it without me. I didn't have a part. Now, Dwight and Hannah both waited for me to speak.

"The potty," I finally said. "They need to sit on the potty before bed."

Dwight and Hannah exchanged glances. "Uh, okay. Yeah, right." Dwight got up and took Brynna into the bathroom. Hannah got a night diaper out for Katie.

"She can do it too," I said.

"Yeah, but I was thinking of just letting her sleep since it's so late," Hannah whispered. "Such a busy day and all." She waited. "What do you think?"

I looked at Katie, limp with sleep and half dressed. I knew she'd only shiver and whine if we put her on the toilet now. "Okay," I said.

"Want to finish this?" Hannah offered me the diaper and moved aside.

"Yes," I said. I took over and had Katie packaged up in a few seconds.

"Gee. You're good!" Hannah whispered.

"I took care of her by myself for three days straight one winter. And Brynna, too." I blurted.

Hannah nodded. "Yes, I've heard that story," she said.

"I wanna hear the story," Brynna mumbled as Dwight brought her back to her bed. She said *story* one more time as her head touched her pillow. Hannah reached and squeezed my arm. She muffled a laugh.

"They are so funny!" she whispered. That made me smile. And boy, there was something about Hannah—something I liked.

breakfasts and boxes

In the morning I woke like a sloth in the fog. I heard a hammer—no, two—thwacking in the distance. I wondered if I'd missed Dwight at breakfast. Something smelled good.

I sat up. The Littles stood on tiptoes on Katie's junior bed—four wide eyes fixed on me. I grinned and blinked.

"You sleeped good, Oddie?"

"Yes, Katie. Did you?"

"Yes, Oddie."

"Brynna sleeped good too. Honnah maked cakes."

"She means pancakes," Brynna added.

"I smell those cakes," I said. "Did you eat?"

"No, we waited for you." They giggled and begged me to come down off my bunk.

I didn't get a whole lot of privacy in the bath-room that morning—the door wasn't quite right on the hinge and the Littles kept popping in—but I didn't care. On my way back down the hall, I stole a peek into the other bedroom—the one I had not really seen in the darkness the night before. A wide bed was not exactly made, but sort of tossed shut, with a fluffy comforter and pillows here and there. The iron head and foot reminded me of the gates at *Onion* College, but the metal was painted white instead of shiny black. So that's where Dwight and Hannah sleep, I thought.

"Come on for cakes, Oddie." Katie pulled at my hand and Brynna led us down the hall. Hannah greeted us with a satisfied sort of sigh. "Well, look at the three of you," she said. "Who wants the first two pancakes?"

"Give 'em to them," I said. "I can make my own."

"Nope," Hannah said. She put her hands on her hips. "If you wanna make breakfast, you have to be the first one up. This is *my* project."

I raised an eyebrow at her. She broke into that huge smile, laughed and threw her braid off her shoulder. She ladled another scoop of batter onto the griddle. "Dwight will come in for breakfast in a few minutes. Then he'll work until lunch and break early so we can have some fun while you're here, Addie."

"Fun, fun, fun!" Brynna danced.

"We gonna do boxes today, Honnah?" Katie asked.

"Yep, some boxes. Boxes until lunchtime."

"What's boxes?" I said.

"Ahhh, remember I mentioned my paying job?" Hannah asked.

"But it's about boxes?"

"Yep. It's in the base-a-ment," Katie told me.

Boxes, it turned out, was a place for me to shine, *and* earn my keep. The basement was long like a bowling alley with a low ceiling. Shelves ran all the way down both sides to the end and they were filled with handmade crafts. A play area had been set up on a round braided rug right in the center of the room and two tricycles were parked at its edge. There was a small TV set, an easel, a toy basket, a portable CD player and a rope swing hanging from a beam.

"Dwight did a good job, huh?" Hannah nodded at the play space.

"That's Dwight," I said. I looked down the row

of shelves at all the crafted goods. "Do you make everything?" I asked.

"No!" Hannah gasped. "I'm a klutz with a needle and thread and I'd probably be afraid of a jigsaw. I just love art and artists so I try to stick to what I'm good at—I sell their work. I met most of these artists on my way out west, believe it or not." She spread her arms out and let them fall again. "Welcome to the world of mail order!"

Everything was organized with numbered three-by-five cards tacked to the shelf fronts. There was a desk with a computer set up in one corner and another area for boxes, tape and packing materials. Hannah had orders to fill.

"This is the catalog." Brynna wagged the stapled pages at me. "But most of the selling happens at the computer." Brynna seemed so smart to me just then, as she pointed to a table where a computer and printer hummed.

"Right. Off the Internet," Hannah explained. She was already going through a stack of papers from the printer tray. "I keep filling orders right up until December fifteenth and then I'm done until New Year's." She took a breath. "Then I handle returns, get my spring crafts in and we go again."

She crossed her eyes at me.

The setup made me think of Mommers. Even the file boxes were the exact same ones that she had all over the floor back at the trailer. But Hannah's were full.

"Can we start, Honnah?" Katie was jumping up and down. "Wanna show Oddie!" She had a shipping box open on the floor in front of her. A layer of shredded paper was already in the bottom of it.

"Okay. Let's show Addie how we do it." Hannah read an order and called out, "Large box." Katie scuttled forward with her box.

"Got it!" she shouted.

"Item zero-four-six," Hannah called. "Quantity, two."

"That's the muslin snowman ornament," Brynna said. That blew me away. All those crafts and she knew which one it was! She trotted along the shelves, stopped right in front of the snowmen, pulled two off the shelf and brought them to Katie's box.

"Check," said Hannah. "Item zero-six-seven. Quantity, six."

"The red bird cedar pillow," Brynna said. "Size small."

That's when I realized she had it—Brynna had the Love of Learning! Mommers would be so glad! I had something good to tell her when I got back.

"Check!" Hannah called. She watched everything go into the box from the corner of her eye.

I became a "runner" like Brynna and we started filling boxes more quickly. I liked hearing Hannah say, "Check! Check!" She gave one copy of each finished order form to Katie and Katie spiked it on a nail—Dwight's touch, they told me—for Hannah to file later. The second copy went into the packed box. The top half of it was the address label.

"They're so good and so cute. They'll run out of steam after about an hour," Hannah said, leaning toward my ear. "Then they play."

I nodded. "Just as well. We learned about child labor laws when we studied immigration at school last year. I'm glad I was born now, not then."

"Hard life, wasn't it?" Hannah said with a nod.

"Yes," I said. "I'm really proud of them, of all the immigrants. They really had to build their lives from nothing but they did it. They're heroes."

"Heroes. . . ." Hannah took a moment to think. "You're right," she said. "They are heroes. Ya know . . . I have some folk music to share with you—some songs about coming to America. Remind me if I forget," she added, putting her finger in the air. She was already checking the next order.

When the Littles grew bored of doing boxes, they hopped on the tricycles, and Hannah and I kept filling orders on our own. I liked the work. I'd take my order on a clipboard, grab an empty box and go down the row filling it up. As I found each item, I'd slide a three-by-five card under that line on my order form and draw a highlight stripe through it. That kept me straight, and I didn't have to explain to Hannah that I didn't have the Love of Learning. I wasn't fast like Hannah and I didn't know all the numbers like Brynna, but I had a long row of filled boxes at the end of the morning anyway.

I think I would have just stayed there if it had been up to me. I liked the way Dwight and Hannah did things.

"Grrrrrr!" It'd be Dwight—covered in sawdust—on the basement stairs coming down to give horseback rides, monster hugs and woodpecker kisses.

"Break!" It'd be Hannah bringing an armload of coats, saying, "Time to go outside!" We did that every afternoon, no matter what the weather was doing. She said it would sound really bad if anyone ever heard that she and Dwight kept the kids in a basement all day. "Besides, I need to get out of there too. Filling the orders isn't the exciting part. Finding the artists and their crafts is," she told me.

At night they talked about the work that was being done on the inn. That was all business stuff. I tried to practice my flute pieces but I kept stopping to listen to them.

One night, Hannah said, "Can't you get your guys to go weather tight on the north side of the building before the fifteenth?"

Dwight shook his head. "I can try, but I don't see how. The materials were late. Can't we just shoot for the week after? It's not gonna make that much difference, Hannah. I'll put some time in on our own kitchen while we wait."

"Dwight!" Hannah raised her voice and my scalp tingled. "I really wanted to meet schedule on this. We talked about this before. Winter is *here*! And what about the gift shop?" She put her hand on her hip. "I'm counting on opening it by spring even if we haven't got a single room to rent yet. I've gotta let people know this place exists. If they come for the crafts maybe they'll come back for the rooms—*when the rooms are done*." She pushed that last line at him.

"I know. I'm trying." Dwight folded back some stapled papers he was reading. "The millwork is on time," he offered. "So, looks good."

"Okay, okay. But listen, I'm gonna need at least three days *alone in the basement*." She whispered that part and made a desperate face at him. "This is my busy season!"

"Right. I'll call the day care. And I'll help you box orders at night." He looked her in the eye. "Okay?"

Hannah sighed and turned away.

Dwight walked all the way around to face her. With his hands on his hips, he waited. When she looked up, he asked her, "Are we okay?"

She nodded. "Yeah, we're okay."

"You still gonna sign my paycheck this week?"

Hannah lost a laugh. "Yes, you jerk." Then they were hugging.

I let out my breath. Were they done? Was that a fight?

That same night, after we'd all gone to bed, I got up again to use the bathroom. As I passed their room, I heard them talking in low voices.

"Dwight, she is a *great* kid." Hannah sounded insistent. She was right. Brynna was a great kid. She was cute and serious and *smart*.

"She's not mine," Dwight said. "Feels like mine, but isn't." That's when I realized they were talking about me. I hung close to the draped doorway of their room and hoped my breathing wouldn't ripple the plastic sheeting. "I told you, I tried to get custody." My heart pumped. "The judge told me I don't stand a chance because we're not blood. Denise would have to sign Addie over to me."

"So, there's nobody to fight for her? What about Jack? He's blood."

"Jack is . . . I don't know . . . I love the guy but he's old and he's crabby. He's been stepping out of the picture lately. I think he feels helpless."

And Grandio doesn't want a kid, I thought.

"Besides, he and Denise are a terrible mix. As far as custody goes, Denise would have to agree and that'll *never* happen. Unless she screws up again, she keeps Addie." After a moment he said, "It sounds like Denise is trying hard."

"She's done that before, from what you said."

He sighed. "Yeah, I know. Something always happens."

"Maybe we need to try harder," Hannah said.

"God knows, if I could fix it, I would. For now, I send the money and I stay in touch as much as I can. Come on, Hannah. Think my heart doesn't break every time I think of this? I miss her and so do the girls."

"Sorry," Hannah said. "But let's get her up here as often as we can, huh?"

"Definitely." Silence. "Hey, Hannah?"

"Yeah?"

"Get your cold feet off me, will ya?"

Hannah giggled, and I ran tiptoe back to my bunk.

He tried to get custody of me! I must have repeated that in my head a thousand times that night. But I thought of Mommers, too. It would be sad if she were alone. Maybe I just had to be the one to do that for her—be her family. I took forever to fall asleep.

On my last morning there, I was up first. I made scrambled eggs on toast. Hannah came yawning into the kitchen saying, "Hey! You stinker! Ya took away my post!" She sat down and ate her eggs, humming "Umm . . ." with each bite.

Dwight did the dishes. "When's the next school break, Addie?" He turned from the sink. "Anything between now and Christmas?"

"Nothing." I shook my head.

"Oddie," Katie piped up. "I want you all to home again soon."

I laughed. "I know," I said. "I'll try. But don't forget the concert on December twelfth. You're all invited."

a ton of turkey soup

"Addie's back!" Elliot called to Soula. She came up the soda aisle kicking her lawn chair in front of her.

"Fresh off the bus," I cheered. Truthfully, I was sore at Mommers for not meeting me at the corner. I'd been gone four whole days! Her car was not at the trailer so I'd stopped at the minimart instead. "Miss me much?" I did a little twirl with my flute case and paper bag in hand.

"Sure did, Little Cookie. How was the lake?"

"Never saw it, but I had a great time," I said. "I learned about mail order."

"No kidding?" Soula said.

"Ah, retail by snail," Elliot said. I grinned at his rhyme.

"I'd be interested in a business like that," Soula said.

"Your plate is full, my girl," Elliot said.

"What happened here while I was gone?" I asked, looking around.

"Well"—Elliot thought for a second—"we got a delivery of ice scrapers on Friday. The soda machine had to be serviced, and regular went up another three cents per gallon. And . . ."—he squinted to look out the front window—"I think one of the mannequins at the Heads and Roses sprouted turkey feathers."

I laughed. "How are you feeling, Soula?"

"Not-so, not-so," she said, which I'd figured out meant it wasn't a bad day but that probably yesterday had been better. "Six down, two to go," she said. She wagged a finger in the air; the painted nail gleamed pink.

"That's good," I said. "You're almost done."

While we were talking, Elliot pushed a box across the floor. He straddled it and slit the top with his utility knife. He pulled a bag of birdseed out of the carton. Seed spilled out onto the floor in a perfect hill. I gulped. He swore under his breath and looked at the empty bag in his hand.

He and Soula looked at each other. Then they both said, exactly together, "Never open the birdseed delivery with a knife." They laughed.

"Why do we always forget that?" Soula asked.

"Because we only get seed once a year," Elliot reminded her.

"Right, each November," said Soula. "Ah, what are we gonna do with this?" She toed the floor near the mound of seed.

"Well, we could toss it out back and see who comes," I said. "Or we could bag it up and sell it for small animals like— Oh gosh! I gotta go check on Piccolo!" I started for the door. "Bye! I'll see you tomorrow after school!" I hurried outside, ran to the street, looked both ways as fast as I could and crossed. Mommers' car was still not out front. I set my bag and the flute down on the step and tried the door. Locked. I shook the handle hard with both hands. No luck. I poked around the front step, under the mud mat and in any little crack or cranny I could find, hoping she'd left the key. Nothing.

I thought about heading back to the minimart, where I could just watch for Mommers' car to pull up. It'd be warmer in there and I'd have something to do. No! I had to try to see Piccolo. I went around to the end of the trailer where my bunk was. I dragged a cinder block up to the window and I stood on it. Cupping my hands against the glass, I looked in. All I could make out was the shape of the cage and the little mound of torn-up tissues inside that was Pic's sleeping nest.

"Piccolo?" I called at the window. Then I tapped. Something in the nest might have moved—a little—but I couldn't be sure. "Pic!" I called again.

I heard a roar—the train above me. I closed my eyes and gripped the little metal window ledge. Still, the gust nearly sucked me off the cinder block. I listened to the clack-clacking sound running away down the tracks.

"Addie! Hey, Addie!"

I opened my eyes. "Oh! Mommers!" I jumped off the block and ran to meet her. She was twisting up her face at me.

"What in the heck were you doing?" she asked.

"I couldn't get in," I said.

"Oh, well, here." She dug into her purse and handed me the key. "Open up da-dump, da-dump-

dump!" she sang. "Then come back out and help me."

I stuck the key in the lock but waited to turn it. "Hey, Mommers?"

"Yeah?"

"Did you remember Piccolo while I was gone?" I made my whole body stiff, trying to wish up good news.

"The rat? Yeah, I remembered. Sheesh!"

"Phew!" I turned the key and went inside.

I tossed my bag and my flute on my bed and hurried to Pic's cage. The nest wiggled. Then up came Piccolo's nose. She sniffed, then she opened two squinty black eyes. She was fine!

Mommers had piled a mountain of hamster food into one corner of the cage and had put an empty cottage cheese container filled with water in beside it.

"Hmm." Mommers came up beside me to peer into the cage. "Little dust ball didn't finish his Thanksgiving supper," she mumbled.

I laughed and put my arm around her. "It's a *she*. And she doesn't know about Thanksgiving."

"Guess not! *She* should be on her back with those little drumsticks in the air. You know, in a food coma!" Mommers threw her hands up and laughed. She grinned at me and gave me a squeeze. "So, how was your big adventure?"

"Great," I said. "But I missed you."

"How are my babies? Did they ask about me?"

"Sure did. The second we got to Grandio's," I said.

"Good. I don't want my girls to forget about me just 'cause Dwight takes them miles away. How was it up there anyway?"

"Oh! Mommers—" I hesitated. "It was all right," I said. I added a shrug.

"And Dwight's all moved in at that Hannah chick's place? What did I hear? A mansion or something?"

"Yes," I said. "It's gonna be an inn. But it's only partway finished now. I mean, they are working on it. It has good bones," I finally said.

"Bones," Mommers scoffed. "Dwight always says that about the hellholes he works on." She let out a laugh. Then she stared off into space for a few seconds. "Well, good for them, I guess. Come on, now. You were gonna help me with the stuff in my trunk."

I followed Mommers out to her car and she

popped open the trunk. She lifted out a bag of groceries and lowered it into my arms.

"Ugh! What's in this?" I said. I hefted the bag toward the trailer door.

"Five pounds of potatoes, two pounds of onions, two pounds of carrots and a big bag of frozen peas," Mommers said. I could tell by her voice that she was struggling with her own big package of something behind me. She practically chased me into the trailer. She dropped her cargo and pushed it across the floor.

"What is it?" I asked, looking at the big plastic garbage bag.

"Turkey carcasses! Two big ones! I'm gonna make a pot of turkey soup." She began sliding her file boxes and office supplies out of the way. It wasn't easy; she ended up loading most of the office supplies onto her own bed in the Luxury Suite.

"Where did you get the turkeys?"

"Soup kitchen," she said. She stopped for a second and let out a loud laugh. "Can you believe that? A soup kitchen that didn't need all their carcasses for soup! Of course, there must have been twenty turkeys there."

"When were you at the soup kitchen?"

"For Thanksgiving," she said. She squinted as she turned on the naked light bulb over the kitchen sink. "God, I hate that thing," she mumbled. She started to fill our stockpot with water. "See, it didn't work out—having dinner with Pete, I mean. He had to cover a family commitment. So, I went to work at the soup kitchen. Boy, did they love me! I might do it every year."

"Oh," I said. "This is gonna be a lot of soup for two."

She shook her head. "Well . . . we could . . . I don't know. We'll freeze it. Whatever. I got these turkeys and I'm gonna use 'em." She started to work on the two carcasses, pulling them apart and cracking them down so they'd fit in the pot. She flicked the burner on and speared the bag of onions with a knife. She lifted it in the air and let it fall onto the counter. "Now, *you* need to clean out Stinky the Wonder Rat's cage, my girl. Chop, chop," she said. She pushed the knife blade through an onion and began slicing it into little pieces.

While Mommers chopped, I let Piccolo out onto my bunk so I could clean her cage. A lot of hamster dirt piled up in four days but it never bothered me. Even Piccolo's pee smelled all right to me; the damp pine shavings smelled woodsy. I brushed them into a paper bag and rolled it shut. I spread fresh chips into the cage and tore some fresh tissues just to get her started on a new sleeping nest. I always felt a little bad destroying Pic's cozy bed every time I cleaned the cage, but she seemed to like rebuilding it. I caught her in my hands. We nosed each other for a minute, then I let her wriggle back into her cage.

The trailer began to fill with good cooking smells. Mommers finished chopping onions and moved on to potatoes. While she worked, I practiced my flute. I worked my way through the pieces we'd chosen for the Stage Orchestra performance until I got each one completely right at least once.

"Sounds good, Addie," Mommers said. She stopped a moment, knife raised, looking at our calendar. She flipped from November to December using the tip of the blade. "That concert is coming up soon, isn't it?"

"Twelve days." I put my flute into its case and snapped the lid shut.

"Phew-wee! We gotta get you outfitted." She slit

open a bag of carrots. "Black on bottom, white on top, right?"

"Uh-huh," I said. "It should be easy. I can stop at the Salvation Army Store on my way home from school one day and see what they have."

"Right," said Mommers.

Later, I opened my vocabulary notebook and sat up in my bunk with Webster's open across my knees. The train went by again and rocked us. There was something homey about it, like the trailer was a big old cradle and we were tucked in for the night.

"Getting hungry?" Mommers asked.

Just those two words added to the goodness.

"Yep," I said. "Smells great, Mommers." Then I looked at Piccolo. She was in one corner of her cage. She had already begun to make a new nest.

from good to bad

On December 1 I had one of those days when everything goes from good to bad and back again all day long—almost like my life was on a switch.

In the morning, I got up on my own. Mommers was still sleeping. There was one last slice of the extra-thick raisin bread left—my favorite. I put it in the toaster. While the toaster hummed, I dug through the clean laundry pile looking for the one pair of my underwear that still had good elastic in the legs—the pair that didn't creep up all day. My toast got stuck and burned while I was still looking for the underpants. I had to carry the toaster outside (I was still in my bathrobe) because it was smoking like a factory. A trucker was sitting there at the light and he started laughing when he saw me.

"Oh big deal," I mumbled to myself. "Burnt toast happens to everyone." When I came back inside, I found the good pair of underpants stuck—static cling—to the sweater I was planning to wear. That was double good. I was saved from an all-day wedgie *and* the embarrassment of showing up at school with a pair of panties stuck to my back.

Next, I turned the calendar to December. That was good too. I like the first day of just about anything. But there in the trailer, on the first day of December, our calendar fell off the hook and hit the floor with a loud crack. Mommers yelled from her room for me to be quiet. I tiptoed into the bathroom and what do you know—I'd gotten my first period. I had to look twice but there it was, a little pinkish red splotch right in the middle of my good underpants. "Oh my gosh!" I whispered to myself. For some reason the whole idea of being that grown-up made me grin—just for a second. I went on whispering to myself. "Gotta do something here. Gotta take care of this. Oh, and I ruined my only good pair of underpants! Darn!"

I went to the door of Mommers' bedroom and whispered her name.

"No, no, no!" She pulled a pillow over her head.

"Be quiet!" she moaned. She lay still then, like she'd gone back to sleep.

I went over to her and shook her shoulder a couple of times. Finally, she opened one eye and looked at me.

"Mommers, I just got my period."

Mommers sat up and blinked. "I knew it! I was right! I knew you'd get it before Christmas! See that?"

I nodded. "Yeah. I need some stuff. Pads. And, Mommers, I *really* need new underwear. Can I get some when Dwight's money comes? That's soon, right? Oh, and speaking of Dwight, don't tell him about this, okay?"

Mommers laughed. "Dwight's so checked out. That man knows nothing when it comes to women. And you just reminded me, that money is *late*," she added. She threw her pillow aside and rolled out of bed.

"It's just the first of December," I said. "It always comes around the first."

"Yeah, well, we'll see," Mommers said. She went into her closet and brought out all kinds of pads. She tossed them out onto her bed. Then she called like a ringmaster at a circus, "Try one, try 'em all! Step right up, little woman!" I started laughing. "And here . . ." She took a second to open her dresser. "Here's a new pair of undies, shrunken down at the fine establishment next door. Just your size!" She looped the waistband on her thumb and slingshot them at me. I grabbed the panties out of the air. They were blazing red, but pretty plain otherwise. I was glad about that. I grabbed a pad from the bed and headed for the bathroom.

"Make sure you take a few pads to school," Mommers called after me, "You're gonna need 'em." I heard her yawn and flop back onto her bed.

"I know, I know," I said.

I knew because of Helena. She'd already had a couple of periods. One day, it *surprised* her—by coming in the middle of math class. *Surprised*—that's what Nurse Sandi had said when we'd arrived at the health office. I always figured *surprises* were things like birthday gifts, and good grades on math tests. Anyway, Helena had to keep going to see Nurse Sandi that day so her *surprise* wouldn't turn into an accident. I bundled half a dozen pads into my backpack. Mommers had fallen back to sleep by the time I left the trailer.

School went okay that day. The only *surprise* I got was when Ms. Rivera rushed up to me in the hall first thing in the morning and said she was giving me a little solo part in the holiday concert.

"Is it a stand-up-in-front-of-everyone solo?" I asked.

She laughed. "You can stay seated if that's more comfortable for you. I want you to play a few measures in 'I Wonder as I Wander.' Since it's a carol, I think the voice of your flute would be lovely for it."

"Thanks," I said. "It's just that I never practice standing up." That was only half the truth, of course. I figured if I got nervous and flubbed up, at least I'd be sitting low and no one would really be sure who the lousy flute player was.

"Can you imagine," I said to Helena and Marissa later that day. "I'd be black on bottom, white on top and red in the face!" We started laughing.

My day seemed to be evening out by the end of school—no accidents. I stopped at the minimart, where Soula was having a better day after two bad ones.

"Seven down. One to go!" she sighed.

"We've got good news all around," Elliot said. He waved a copy of the *Gazette*. I squinted and saw that it was turned back to the entertainment section.

"Rick stopped by. Good review for Numbskull Dorry's," he said, grinning. "Good reviews are everything in the restaurant business."

"Weee-hah!" I said. "And I have news too. I got a solo in the holiday concert."

"Hey, hey, hey!" Soula cheered. "Good day on the corner. Calls for a pie celebration, don't you think?" I took my cue and put three apple pie pockets into the microwave. Elliot read the review to us, slowing over words like *unmatched* and *exquisite,* and phrases like *unadulterated goodness.* Soula made a joke that he was memorizing the entire article. He held the paper to his chest and grinned.

"Not bad for a pub, huh?" he said.

"Elliot, how come you don't work at the restaurant with Rick?" I asked.

Soula laughed out loud, then tried to squelch it. Elliot rolled his eyes. He looked up at the ceiling and let out a long whistle. "Most couples learn that there are some things you can do together and some things you can't."

"Yeah?" I said.

"Tell her what you really mean," Soula nudged.

Elliot squinted at me. "Rick and I would fight if I had my fingers in his pub biz," he said. "Plain and simple. We can't even hang wallpaper together unless someone else comes over to make sure we remain civil."

"Oh," I said. "And you just know that about each other?"

Soula exhaled a chuckle. "Well, they found out," she said softly. Elliot nodded in agreement.

I sat there eating my apple pie, thinking about Dwight and Hannah. I thought they probably *could* hang wallpaper together. They were good together, I thought, in a way that Mommers and Dwight never had been.

We were getting into short days. The sun was way low at four o'clock when I crossed the street and climbed the trailer steps. I stopped to shake the crumbs out of the toaster, which was still sitting there from that morning. I coiled the cord and went inside. Mommers wasn't home but I could tell she'd been there for lunch: her soup bowl was in the sink. We were still eating the turkey soup from the carcasses Mommers had brought home from the soup kitchen. The freezer was packed with it—not a bad thing.

I did the dishes and was just finishing when I heard Mommers pull up. She followed a big-handled shopping bag into the trailer. She looked good shaking back her bangs. Her cheeks were pink and she smiled.

"Got something here!" She raised the shopping bag.

"Oh yeah?"

Mommers giggled. She yanked a box out of the bag and threw it onto the table. She shook the lid off and spread back the tissue paper. She drew out a long dress. It was skinny and black with big white ruffles running all around the chest. The straps were just little strings—the kind Mommers liked to wear when she had somewhere fancy to go.

"Whaddaya think?" she asked breathlessly. The dress looked like a piece of black licorice with whipped cream on top but I didn't want to say so.

"Uh, well, where are you going?"

She cocked her head at me. "*I'm* not going any-where. *You* are!"

"Me? Where am I going?"

"To the concert. Black on bottom, white on top!" She made a sweeping gesture with her hand.

"Uh . . . Mommers," I said slowly, "isn't that a *lady's* dress?"

"Yeah. What are *you*?" She cocked her hip.

"W-well, but I was thinking of a skirt with tights and a turtleneck—"

"Addison! That's boring! Go try this on! Use my room."

I hesitated.

"Go!" She pushed the dress at me.

I did it—I wriggled into the dress. But it felt all wrong. "These ruffles make me feel like I have to keep my arms up in the air," I called. "And it's itchy. And my bra is showing. And I have this sort of sausage roll at my belly."

"Let me see."

I stepped out.

"Oh! It's gorgeous! Suck your gut in." She reached to give me a slap.

I grunted and adjusted a strap. I tugged on my underwear. "This isn't gonna work." I shook my head.

"Yeah it is. It's perfect." Mommers lit a cigarette

and eyed me a moment.

"Mommers, everyone is wearing simpler stuff than this. It's too fancy and too clingy," I added.

"I think it looks great," she said. I knew I was in major trouble. Mommers had that look on her face, that I've-made-up-my-mind look. I sagged against the doorjamb. How could this be happening? "Come here," she said, taking a clip out of her hair. She pulled my hair up off my neck, twisted it and caught it up in the clip. "There," she said. "Wow! You could be sixteen."

"Exactly!" I said, louder than I meant to. "Mommers, I'm sorry but I don't like the dress. Not for this concert and not for me."

Mommers waited a few seconds, then said, "Too bad, Addison. Black on bottom, white on top. This is it."

A knock on the trailer door saved me from whatever I might have done next. I ran for cover in the Luxury Suite. Mommers answered the door and I heard Dwight's voice.

"Dwight!" I said. I came back out without thinking. There he was holding a big white poinsettia in his arms and an envelope between two fingers. He was looking right at me—chin on the floor.

"Whoa!" he said. And then again: "Whoa!" His eyes went huge. He looked like he was going to tip over backward. "I . . . uh . . . I ended up in Schenectady to see a supplier today and . . . I thought I'd bring the money by in person. You playing dress-up or something?"

"Nope," Mommers said sharply. She took the envelope from him and poked through the contents. "I bought it for her. She has a concert coming up."

"What? Denise! Hey, you might wanna think this one through a little," he said. He looked me up and down. "I mean, Jaysus! Jaysus!" He shook his head.

I shut my eyes. *Please let me be dressed in a huge sweatshirt when I open my eyes.* No such luck.

"Well, she's a *woman* now," Mommers said.

"Mommers! Don't!" I begged.

"A woman?" He looked back and forth between us.

"Take a wild guess, Dwight," Mommers said, grinning.

"Mommers, you promised not to tell!"

A second ticked by. "Oh," said Dwight. "Really? I mean, *Oh! Wow!*"

"That's brilliant, Dwight. Can you say that again?" Mommers smirked.

"Stop it, Denise." Dwight fumbled. "Hey, Addie, way to go, kid." He shrugged and covered his chin with his free hand. I tried to ignore how uncomfortable he was.

"Dwight," I pleaded. "What about the dress?" I shook my hands at my sides and thought, *Help me!*

He set the poinsettia down on our table. "Uh . . . yeah. Yeah, Denise, I don't think the dress is right and Addie's uncomfortable."

"It fits her perfectly."

"Well, that may be true. But"—he shook his head—"Addie is a kid. She's twelve, Denise. This is . . . this is . . ." He looked at me again, and blew a puff of breath into his bangs. "Jaysus, I don't know what this is."

I folded my arms across my chest and tried to stare at my feet. The dress ruffles brushed my nose. Why did Dwight have to be such a doofus?

"Addie, listen, I'm sorry," he said. He reached to pick up my chin. I wriggled away. "I agree with you, honey. The dress is too old for you."

"Well, I think she looks gorgeous," Mommers concluded. "Besides, you have no say in the matter."

She turned to Dwight and gave him a straight-line smile. "Do ya, now?"

That was it for me and I knew it. She was right. There was no other person in charge of me. No one to say, "Don't make her wear that dress."

"Just quit looking at me." I pushed past them both and dragged myself, in my licorice dress, up into my bunk. I pulled my curtain, but not all the way.

Mommers said, "Well, look what ya did this time, Mr. Perfect Papa! Got her all upset!"

"Hey!" Dwight pointed a finger at her. "Don't be so quick handing off the Amateur Parenting Award. . . ." He stopped. "Ya know what, Denise? Forget it. Just forget it. I'm not even gonna go there. Addie, I'll call you later. Oh, and Hannah sent this CD for you. She said you'd know what it is." I heard him set it down. He peeked into my curtain. I backed up where he couldn't see me. "I'll call," he repeated. Then he left.

Mommers and I didn't talk about the dress anymore. In fact, we didn't talk about anything at all. I changed and we ate turkey soup on toast and Mommers watched *Jeanette for the Judgment*. I had just finished my homework when Dwight called.

154

"Addie, I didn't mean to embarrass you," he said.

"I know," I said.

"I can hardly hear you."

I sniffed, blinked my burning eyes and tried to be louder. "I said I know."

"I'm not used to little girls growing up. Don't know anything about it. Mr. *Duh*, that's me."

"Never mind."

"I'm gonna be at your concert, ya know? I'm bringing the Littles and Hannah too, if that's okay with you."

"Uh-huh." I thought about the dress again and I let a spill of tears loose. I wiped my nose on my sleeve. Mommers looked at me and rolled her eyes like I was being ridiculous. Then she went back to watching *Jeanette*.

I didn't say much more to Dwight. He tried to congratulate me on being a woman but it came out all messed up when he got flustered. "Forget it," I told him. Then I said good-bye. When he hung up I was sorry I hadn't been nicer to him. He'd tried to stick up for me. I hadn't thanked him for that.

I blew my nose and climbed into my bunk for

the night. Mommers kept giggling at something on the TV. I peeked out of my curtain and saw her put a cigarette out in the dirt of the new poinsettia pot. I curled into a ball like Piccolo, hoping I'd fall asleep fast.

willing to bloom

December twelfth is one of the shortest days of the year, but it was a long day at school. We were waiting for seventh period, when the Stage Orchestra was to perform the holiday concert for the staff and students. It was like a dress rehearsal, only without the dress—a good thing, if you asked me. Finally, our principal announced that the members of the Stage Orchestra should assemble in the auditorium. I followed Robert and Helena down the hall.

I'm not sure but I think we played the best we ever had. Nobody sounded flat or squeaky. Nobody lagged; the tempo was right on each piece. For my solo part, I fixed my eyes on Ms. Rivera. (One advantage to not being able to read the music is that you can keep your eyes on the conductor.) I came in perfectly on her cue and didn't miss a note.

Ms. Rivera was happy; she turned to face all the musicians while the audience was still clapping (and clapping, and clapping). Her pretty red lips formed an exaggerated *Thank you* to all of us. A rush of blood warmed my chest.

Afterward, the stage buzzed as everyone put their instruments away. They were all excited about the *real* concert, yet to come. I stayed in my chair for a while. I pulled the swab through the flute a few more times than I needed to. I could never stop reminding myself that the flute should have been returned to Borden School. I also flashed on my terrible dress over and over again.

"Addie?" I blinked and looked up at Helena. "What's the matter? It went well, don't you think?" Her voice rose so cheerfully I had to smile.

"Yes. But I was just thinking . . . well." I waited. "Part of what I was thinking is that I wish we didn't need to do the concert again. I wish we were done. I don't want to come back tonight to play for the parents and grandparents." Or stepparents. "Besides, what are the chances we'll all be that good again?"

"Addie?" Helena squinted at me.

My eyes burned. "No, really. What are the

158

chances Robert will leave enough bow to hold the long notes on 'Song of Winter' again? He's been having trouble with that." Helena nodded slightly. "And me. Will I really hit my solo twice in one day?" I shook my head. "It's no big deal, I guess." I fumbled with the sections of my flute as I tried to put it in the case. I'd broken it down a thousand times but I was getting it all wrong. I switched the sections around again. Helena sat down next to me.

"My dress for tonight is awful," I whispered.

"Oh, you got a *dress*? I have a hand-me-down skirt. It's too short to be long and too long to be short. I look dorky in it." She snorted a laugh.

"My mother bought me a dress," I said. "It's . . . it's a grown-up dress. It's a gown, like a model would wear."

"Oh." Helena poked her bottom lip out.

"It's tight. The straps are skinny. My bra shows. Oh, Helena, I don't think I can bear to wear it."

"What are you gonna do?" Helena asked.

I shrugged. "Nothing. My mother says I have to wear it."

"Can you wear a sweater over the top?"

I thought about that. "I don't think so. There's this ruffle around the chest. It looks like a tutu." I wondered if I could somehow stuff it all under a sweater. Then again, I knew Mommers wouldn't go for that. "I think I'm stuck," I said.

"Well, never mind," Helena said. "It doesn't matter what you wear." She put her hand on my shoulder. "You'll be awesome tonight. All of us will be."

Helena stuck with me on the way home. We walked past the gates of *Onion* College together. The trees were bare but the weather was mild that day. We'd had a few good snows and the streets were filled with puddles that'd freeze in the night. The shops and houses along Nott Street were decorated for the holiday. Helena and I pointed them out to each other as we walked. The window of the Tibetan shop was filled with satiny ropes of brass bells, paper lanterns and stacks of embroidered prayer rugs like always. The man in the store switched on a set of multicolored lights just as we strolled by and the whole window shone like one big ornament.

The guys at Hose Company No. 6 were busy. One guy stood there with his yellow rubber coat on, arms spread wide, while another fireman sprayed the mud off him with a hose.

"There. That's what I need," I said, nudging

Helena. "A big Hose Number Six raincoat."

Helena covered a laugh with her hand. "Hard to play the flute in," she giggled. "Go ahead, Addie. Ask him if you can borrow it!"

"Oh, Helena!" I laughed.

Just then the guy in the coat looked up at us and flapped his arms. I gave Helena a shove to move her along the street. I knew we were going to start cracking up again if we stayed.

At the Goose Hill Barber Shop, where we always split up, Helena said, "You will come tonight, right? You won't skip out?"

I stood looking at the beautiful tree inside the barber shop window. Several red blossoms, as big as paper plates, had opened up on it, and the barber had strung hundreds of tiny white lights through the branches. I had described the tree to Soula one day, and had asked her what kind it could be. She'd told me, "Sounds like a Chinese hibiscus, Cookie. Terrific indoor tree, and willing to bloom in conditions it was never meant to encounter."

Willing.

"I'll be there," I told Helena. "I know people are counting on me."

twists and turns

The plan was for Mommers to take me to the school that night. Dwight and Hannah and the Littles were supposed to arrive on their own. Then we were all going to Numbskull Dorry's for dessert. That was something to be nervous about right there; Mommers was about to meet Hannah. But I knew if we got through that, and if I got through my music okay, the night could be fun. Besides, I had decided that Helena was right: the concert was going to be great and I couldn't let a bad dress ruin it for me. I made a choice to un-grump.

Mommers wasn't at the trailer when I got home from school. Two hours later, at six o'clock, she still wasn't there. I needed to be at the school at seven, so I figured I should eat. I'd taken a container of turkey soup from the freezer earlier and I dumped it, still partially frozen, into a pan on the stove.

I ate my soup, peeking out the front window every once in a while to see if Mommers was coming. At six thirty, I rinsed my bowl and figured I'd better get ready. I took the world's fastest shower, using most of the time to shave my armpits—very carefully. I stepped into the dress and yanked it up hard, hoping it would split in two. (It didn't.) I tucked my bra straps down inside the ruffle.

"Piccolo," I said, stopping by her cage, "be glad you came to the world with fur." She started a run on her wheel.

I looked in the mirror. My shoulders looked naked. I remembered Helena's idea about the sweater and decided to try it even if it would make Mommers mad. I looked through my own things, came up empty and headed for Mommers' room. There was a white cardigan with pearly buttons in her drawer. I pushed my arms into the sweater. I wrestled the ruffle flat and got all the buttons closed. "Ha! Trapped it!" I said, and Piccolo stopped running to look at me.

I went to the mirror once more. "This is all

wrong," I sighed. The flattened ruffle showed through the sweater and looked like some kind of strange roadkill. The sweater rode up too short on me because of the ruffle, which was trying to spring back to full fluff. I pulled down on the sweater hem so many times it began to lose shape. I knew I had Helena beat on the dorkiness scale no matter what her skirt looked like. And talk about *itchy*! With all that netting rubbing my skin, I felt like I was being sanded. On the other hand, I was happy to be covered up. "White on top, black on bottom." I did a little side-to-side glance in the mirror and talked myself into thinking that I looked okay.

I grabbed my Fresh Whisper and reached under the sweater—couldn't let that ruffle out—and loaded my pits. I brushed my hair, then my teeth, and checked the clock. Six fifty. I shuffled into a pair of black plastic clogs, my only nonsneaker shoes.

"We'll have to fly to be there by seven now," I told Pic. "And"—I raised a finger and grinned— "Mommers will be too late to make me change . . . if she ever shows. Gosh, she has to show." I put my coat on and looked out the picture window. No sign of the blue car.

At seven fifteen, I felt hotter than a prairie fire. I'd been buttoned up in all my layers for twenty long minutes. "Oh, Mommers! Come on! Come on!" I wriggled and clenched the handle of the flute case hard in my hand. Finally, it hit me, she wasn't coming. I was going to miss the concert.

The phone rang.

"Addie?" Dwight spoke loudly, like he couldn't hear well. In the background I could hear the members of the Stage Orchestra tuning their instruments. "Where are you?" he shouted.

Well, think about that, Dwight, I thought to say. *Where did you call?* That's what Mommers would have said to him. I bit my lip.

"Mommers must have forgotten," I said.

"How the heck— Hold on," he said. Dwight was talking to somebody. Hannah? No. He had Ms. Rivera there with him.

"I should've walked," I said, knowing it was too late now.

"Addie, be ready! I'm coming!" I heard a click.

Dwight came screeching up in front of the trailer minutes later and I hopped into Hannah's car. (The truck was too small for everyone.) He flashed a white smile at me. "Hiya!"

I grinned back. "Hiya," I said.

I assembled my flute in the car as we roared up Nott Street. I ran into the school at the backstage door, which was propped open for air, with Dwight on my heels. I peeked into the auditorium. The house lights were still up. I caught a look at a few faces in the front row.

"Oh God!" I gasped. I backed out so fast I stepped on Dwight's boots. "We have to leave!" I grabbed his arm.

"What? Addie, come on. They waited for you!"

Ms. Rivera was turned toward me, a nervous smile on her lips.

"Dwight! I can't," I whispered. I dug my fingers into him.

"Ow!"

"We *have* to leave," I said. I pulled him back out toward the parking lot. My heart pounded. I could hardly breathe. "It's Mrs. Sylvester," I said, still gripping his jacket. "She's the music teacher from my old school. She's here!"

"So?" Dwight's face was all twisted up. My bottom lip started to quiver.

"The flute. She knows I never returned it. Dwight, I mean it. I can't go in."

Dwight went inside just long enough to flag Ms. Rivera. I guess he told her to start the concert without me.

"I'm sorry," I said when he came back. I had already disassembled the flute and was snapping down the lid. The sound of our opening piece poured from the stage door. It was beautiful—and crushing. "I know you went to a lot of trouble to be here. And to get me here," I choked.

"No, no, no. Never mind that." Dwight reached into his pocket, but since he was in his fancy clothes he didn't have a handkerchief. He pulled his sleeve down over his hand and wiped my face first, then my nose. He pulled me inside his jacket and stood there hugging me. Hannah came around the building from the main entrance within minutes, one Little on each arm.

"Are you guys all right?" she asked. She dropped my sisters' hands and they ran to me.

"Why you didn't play, Oddie?" Katie wanted to know.

"What happened?" Brynna stared at me. Poor Brynna. I wished she were still little like Katie. We couldn't just blow her off anymore by telling her part of the truth or plunking a dish of ice cream in front of her.

"The . . . the flute," I lied. "I have a problem with the flute."

"Right," said Dwight. "We need to do something about the flute."

Hannah and Brynna looked completely puzzled still.

Dwight brought his hands together in a loud clap that I think startled even him. "Why don't we go for a drive, look at Christmas lights, and we'll end up over at Numbskull Dorry's like we were planning."

"Yippee!" Katie's happy breath made a cloud in the chilly air.

"That way Mommers can still catch up with us there," Dwight added.

Mommers. I fumed at the mention of her. Anger roared up inside of me, then faded in a sick feeling.

"Can you take me back to the trailer first?" I asked. "I want to change."

. . .

Mommers arrived at Numbskull Dorry's Pretty Good Pub Food in a frantic flurry of swear words. Her hair was a mess, like tumbled hay. I watched her wide eyes narrow as she focused on me.

"Where were you?" she fired at me. "I get to the concert expecting to see you on that stage and . . . Is this about the dress, Addison?" She stared at my clothes—jeans and a sweatshirt. I felt surprisingly calm. "Where *is* the dress?" she spat.

The silence went long. Finally, Dwight stood up.

"Come on, Denise. Been a few twists and turns tonight," he said in a low and gentle voice.

"Twists and turns— I'll say," I mumbled.

"The concert," Mommers said, looking at me. "What happened?"

I shrugged.

"We had a little problem with the flute," Dwight said. He touched my shoulder. "Didn't we, Addie, girl?"

"Yes," I said.

"Well . . . what? Is it broken? We'll get it fixed," Mommers said. She combed her hair out of her face with her fingers.

"It's not that simple," I mumbled.

"What are you telling me, Addison? Can't somebody just *tell* me?"

"Let's get you a piece of pie, huh? Sit down." Dwight offered Mommers a chair, his hand on her back. "By the way, this is Han—"

Mommers threw Dwight off. He moved away from her.

I looked around me. Hannah sat pulling her lips in between her teeth. Katie leaned close to Hannah, and Brynna sat twisting her napkin in her fingers while she stared into her lap.

This is going nicely, I thought.

I cleared my throat. "Mommers, I waited for you at the trailer," I said, looking her in the eye. "I waited *forever*."

the counting-on part

Mommers stared back at me, not speaking. Hannah was making tiny throat-clearing noises. She wrapped Katie with one arm. Her other hand was open over Brynna's knee. Dwight waited. He did that a lot—waited like a circus guy who has the job of *catching* but the net was never big enough.

Mommers and I stayed locked on each other. Then she did it—blinked, like a person waking. She dropped her head into her own hand, her thumb and finger pressing her temples. I knew that pose. That meant she was done with the angry stuff. I sat back in my chair, still watching her. She looked like a car out of gas on a hill.

"Denise? Everything all right?" Dwight asked. Mommers slowly let herself into a chair. Her purse hit the floor at her side.

"I'm just . . . just so . . . I don't know . . . tired," she said. "And I was worried. I couldn't find you all." She looked from person to person at the table. "None of you were at the school."

"Well, here we are," Hannah said softly. "You've found us now." Mommers looked at her—no particular expression. Hannah forced a smile and I thought I should pull her aside and tell her—tell her what? Not to bother?

"You're Hannah," Mommers said, focusing now.

"Yes. Nice to meet you," Hannah said. Gentle smile.

Mommers' gaze seemed to trace the outline of Hannah and my little sisters as they leaned together. Katie's pink fingers curled around a roll in Hannah's sweater. Brynna rubbed her ear against Hannah like a cat passing a couch. I felt sorry for Mommers then. Those were *her* little girls.

Katie broke the silence. "Mommers, I gotted the clown head ice cream." She turned her bowl around to show Mommers. "See?"

"Nice, sweetie." Mommers' voice was quiet.

"And Brynna, honey, what did you get?"

"It's just a sundae." Brynna dropped her head, started messing with her napkin again. Her fudge sundae puddled around the spoon in the dish.

"You gonna finish? It looks like soup." Mommers smiled. But Brynna wouldn't look up. She just kept twisting that napkin.

"We seed Christmas lights," Katie piped.

"Did you now? Any snowmen? Any reindeer?" Mommers asked.

And so it went for the rest of the night. Katie kept everything light and sweet. But I wondered what would happen when she grew up—like Brynna. We'd be this whole family of napkin twisters.

At home that night, I curled up in my bunk and felt terrible. I had *missed the concert*. I'd let everyone down. I wrapped my arms around my pillow and squeezed it hard. I'd been looking forward to December twelfth for weeks. Now it was over and there was no going back. No going back to the flute either, I decided.

It'll just happen again, I thought. Tonight will happen again.

Not the concert, but something like it. Maybe there would not be a stolen flute again, but there could be another embarrassing dress. Or worse, a ride that never comes. I thought of how Ms. Rivera had waited for me, how the entire Stage Orchestra had waited—*my friends*! But I had run away when they were all counting on me. That was the thing that bothered me most: the *counting-on* part.

I socked my pillow. Even before that night there were other things. I'd quit taking books out of the school library in second grade because they always got lost in the house, lost in the mess. I had fixed that. Every week, when my class went to the library, I made sure I took too long to make my selection. Then there wasn't time for me to check out any more books.

"I used to be smarter!" I whispered in the dark. "I never should have taken that flute in the first place!" I made a plan before I went to sleep. The flute was going back where it belonged.

a frozen good-bye

I came out of the shower the next morning and heard Mommers talking on the phone. "Maybe, Dwight. I'll think about it. I'm not going to give you an answer now. And next time, don't call so early on a Saturday!" She banged the phone into the cradle.

"Sorry I wasn't out to answer it," I said, rubbing my hair with a towel.

Mommers said nothing. She lit a cigarette and pulled her robe around her.

"What did Dwight want?"

"You."

"Really?"

Mommers nodded. "For part of Christmas break."

"Oh." I waited, then said, "Wouldn't that be

good? I mean if it's just for part? Aren't you and Pete going to be working?"

"Like I told Dwight, I'll think about it."

I dropped it there. She was in her "don't press me" mood.

"Hey, Mommers? What are you doing today?" I asked.

"I'm leaving in an hour. I'll be gone awhile. Why?"

"Just wondered," I said.

As soon as Mommers drove away, I bundled into my winter coat, hat and mittens. I was in for a long, cold walk; the weather had turned. I knew I should have boots but I couldn't squeeze into the pair I'd worn last year. My feet had grown into gunboats. I picked up the flute and started out the door. I guess it was about a mile—maybe a little more—to the bridge. The sidewalk was an obstacle course of brown, frozen snow and ice patches. At the crossings, I had to get pushy with the traffic. The flute case rattled at the handle and bumped on my hip as I trotted across the street. I was glad I hadn't taken up the tuba.

I got onto Freeman's Bridge—the footpath—and started across. Down below, the mighty, muddy

Mohawk River had started to freeze. Islands of white ice pushed their way slowly through the water, bumping the banks and getting caught in the flow again. They seemed to try themselves out in empty spots like a giant puzzle wanting to be finished. But except for the ice there wasn't much life on the river in December. Looking down made me dizzy, especially at the center of the bridge. I liked being even just a few steps closer to one side or the other. I set my gaze ahead and listened to my own feet scraping across the steel until I padded onto the packed snow on the other side of the river. I was a secret agent about to make a drop. I swung the flute case in my hand. Nobody would know anything until Monday morning. I hoped I'd never hear anything about it again.

I started to hum the music from the concert while I walked. I hummed all of "Around the World at Christmas Time." Then I switched to the Russian folk piece called "Song of Winter." On "Arrival of the Queen of Sheba," I shimmied and slinked along, thinking of Helena and all our fun. I was going to miss being in the Stage Orchestra, but it was a relief to know that I'd be free of stolen property soon. I held the flute case out in front of me and let it lead me in a wavy pattern as I hummed. I danced past the turn that would've taken me up toward Grandio's farm and kept on going. I did the entire holiday concert in humming, and then I started it again.

Finally, I reached the intersection at Route 50. I had only to cross there, go a short ways on Borden Road and then turn into the school driveway. Easy.

Right. Easy except for the road crew. Two yellow trucks were inching along the parking lot of my old school cleaning up the dirty snow.

"Jeepers," I said right out loud. "Ever hear of taking Saturday off?" The plows pushed scoop after scoop of frozen, filthy snow around two lampposts. I don't think they noticed me. Up near the front entrance, a woman chopped at the ice with a shovel. She never looked up from her work.

My plan was messed up. There was no way I could leave the flute at the front door now. I'd have to wait until they finished. So, I kept walking right onto the play yard. I sat on a swing that creaked in the cold air and kept watch on the driveway, waiting for the trucks to go.

I started to shiver and my toes felt stingy inside my sneakers. The morning had gotten no warmer.

"Leave already!" I complained. "Just leave!" My fingers cramped from holding the flute case. I'll bet an hour went by. Felt like two. Finally, the two trucks bumped away, the woman's shovel rattling around in the back of one. I hiked myself up to the front door of Borden School and set the flute down gently on the rubber mat. I started away, then turned back to look at the slim black case.

"It's been awesome," I said. I raised a hand and waved good-bye to music.

an unexpected meeting

"Move, move, move!" I huffed into the air. I was talking to my own body. I shook my hands and pumped my elbows. All my hinges ached from the cold. "Exercise warms you," I insisted. My breath came out in white clouds. So why wasn't this working? I jogged along the school driveway out to the street begging my body to heat up. I thought of lunch for some crazy reason, maybe because it was lunchtime. Was there still turkey soup at the trailer? That would be good right now. I jogged up to Route 50. There I had to fight the traffic again. One thing about the city is that the drivers watch for pedestrians. But cross the bridge and you're just a speck. There are no crossing lights even where the intersections are busy. I waited and waited while cars buzzed by me. I looked for a clearing and darted across the road. Someone laid on their horn and nearly honked me out of my shoes. I ignored that and jogged on.

Again I heard the horn—same one, for sure. Okay, so whoever he was, he was heading the same way as me and got *two* chances to be rude. "Think I *want* to be walking out here in the freezing cold, buddy?" I was talking to myself again. I tried to pick up speed just to get closer to home. A big car pulled to the side of the road in front of me. It rolled into a narrow parking lot beyond me. I looked at the glowing taillights and squinted. There was something familiar about that car—

"Addie! Come on, Addie!"

I blinked. "Grandio! Hey, Grandio!" I waved, ran on my numb feet to the passenger's door and pulled it open.

"What the heck, girl? Didn't you know it was me? Where you been?" he grumbled.

I plunked myself down on the seat of the warm, warm, wonderful car. "Oh," I sighed. "I just wasn't expecting you. I've been walking, Grandio. Boy, have I been walking."

"Walking? It's twenty-two degrees out this

afternoon, kiddo. And no boots! You must get all your sense from your mother."

I sighed. I tugged off my mittens and put my hands to the blower. It was good to be warm.

I had lunch with Grandio that afternoon. He took me down to his favorite diner, where his friend Jimmy threw the burgers and sandwiches high off the grill when he flipped them. From the booths you could watch the wall behind the big brick chimney and see the food go twirling in the air every once in a while. Back when Mommers and Dwight were still married, Grandio treated us to lunch there almost every Saturday. Jimmy liked to call out silly sayings and all the regulars at the diner would answer him back. He'd call, "Shiver me timbers!" and the diners would call back, "Thar she blows!" The burger would shoot a second later.

"Hey, Grandio," I said, taking off my jacket. "Here we are back at Jimmy's and it's Saturday." I grinned.

"Guess so," Grandio answered. He opened his menu.

"Addie? That you?" Jimmy shot me a bug-eyed look from his place at the grill. "You going to college next year or what?"

I blushed. "Hi, Jimmy. Not quite yet," I said. He went back to his work.

"I wish Brynna and Katie were here today," I told Grandio. "Coming here was always fun." When things were normal, I thought to myself.

Grandio browsed the menu. "Them were better days, girl. Better days," he mumbled. "Over and gone now." He was right, I guess. When our family broke up, all of our patterns broke too, including trips to the diner, including time with Grandio. He couldn't get along with Mommers, not without Dwight there keeping everyone calm.

Jimmy howled from behind the bricks. "Catch it if you can!"

"And feed it to the dogs if ya miss!" I hooted back. I smiled. It felt good to know what was coming next, even if it was just lunch.

When Grandio dropped me off at the trailer, he gave me a twenty-dollar bill.

"What's this for?" I asked.

"For something you want but don't really need," Grandio said, which was pretty sweet of him when I thought of it.

First I checked on the Hamster Pantry—a little shelf in my closet where I kept Piccolo's food. Things looked good there. Soula and Elliot had bagged up the spilled birdseed for her. Mommers had picked up a good-sized box of alfalfa feed last time she'd gone to the grocery store.

I rolled the twenty-dollar bill around my index finger. I could save it all; I knew that. But if Mommers had to borrow it, she might forget to give it back. What did I want?

Hot soup! That's what. And not turkey this time.

Just like Grandio had said, it was something I didn't really need—I'd already had lunch. But I did want it.

"Pic, I'm going across the street," I said. "Be back in a little while."

"Ya know, Little Cookie, I could easily see you having that cup o' soup on the house," Soula said. She was sitting in her lawn chair wearing a long sweater—biggest sweater I'd ever seen. She had given up her plastic sandals, in honor of winter, she'd told me, and now she wore a pair of frog slippers.

"Thanks, but I'm a normal paying customer today." I grinned and handed the twenty-dollar bill to Elliot, who was fiddling with a new telephone behind the register.

"Hang on," he said. "I'm just setting this up and . . . there! That should do it. Emergency numbers are entered," he said.

"Newfangled baloney," Soula mumbled. "I'm no techie, Elliot. I'm not going to be able to work that thing. I told you that."

"All you have to do is lift the receiver," he demonstrated, "and press one button to get help. Number two for fire, number three for police. It's all automatic," he said.

Soula flapped a hand at him. "Junk, junk, junk! We don't need it."

"Excuse me! You sell gasoline. As in 'a highly flammable substance'!" Elliot waved his arms in the air.

"Worrywart!" Soula said. "How many years have we been doing this? And how many fires have we had?"

"You never know," he insisted. "Now pardon me while I wait on my customer." He grinned at me most pleasantly and rang up my soup.

I leaned forward and whispered, "I'm glad you have the new phone." He winked back.

"Did we see you heading out on foot this morning?" he asked as he handed me my change. "You looked like a woman with a mission."

"Yeah," I said. I took a spoonful of soup. "I kinda had to go somewhere." Before they could ask about the flute I said, "And, man, was it cold out there! My grandfather came along and picked me up on my way back home. Boy, was I glad to see him! I think I'm still part Popsicle, though."

"'Tis the season," Elliot said.

"'Tis," Soula agreed with a sigh. "By the way, who has what for holiday plans?" she asked.

"Umm, umm, umm!" I rushed a swallow of my soup. "I *might* have plans! I might be going back up to Lake George to see my little sisters. I'm hoping Mommers will say I can go."

"Again?"

"Hope so," I said. I held up crossed fingers.

"Yeah, yeah," Elliot sighed, "and one of these days you'll go up there and you won't come back." He pouted.

I thought about that. "No. I don't think that'll happen," I said.

"Well, everybody leaves the corner eventually," Elliot said, ducking to peek out the front window.

Soula huffed at him, annoyed. "Stop whining!" she said. "We're still here, aren't we?"

a few gifts before christmas

O n Monday morning Ms. Rivera met me at the school's main entrance. "Addie, come down to the music room with me, will you?"

"Sorry, Ms. Rivera, but I'll get marked tardy." I tried to dodge.

"You have a few minutes. Besides, I've cleared it with your teacher," Ms. Rivera said firmly. I followed her down the hall. She had one of those little hot pots full of water going on the little table next to her desk. She offered me a hot chocolate. I wanted it, of course, but I said no thank you.

"Can you tell me what happened at the holiday concert?"

"Yes, I can," I said. "First, I was just plain running late and I'm real sorry about that. And next, I saw somebody there. She's the music teacher from my old school."

"Mrs. Sylvester?"

"Yes." I was a little surprised. Ms. Rivera seemed to know her.

"And why was that a problem?"

"She . . ." I cleared my throat. "She knew something about me. About the flute I've been playing this year. I didn't want her to see me."

"I don't understand."

I explained that the flute was signed out to me from Borden School. "I should have returned it when we moved," I croaked. "It was kind of stolen," I said. "I'm really sorry I let you down for the holiday concert. I just knew I couldn't play knowing that Mrs. Sylvester was watching me. I don't think my lips would have worked."

"I see." Ms. Rivera smiled slightly and sat back in her chair. She held a cup of coffee in both her hands. "I wish you had told me about the problem before. Mrs. Sylvester is a friend of mine. I think something can be worked out."

The first bell rang and I stood up. "That won't be necessary." I tried to sound very grown-up. "I took the flute back to Borden School this weekend."

"Well, we can get it back, then. Or we can get you a different one," Ms. Rivera said.

Stick to the plan. Stick to the plan.

I thumped the toe of my sneaker on the floor. "You know what, Ms. Rivera? I appreciate that. I really do. And I'd like to play the flute again someday. But to tell you the truth, it's been like a huge weight off my back ever since I returned that instrument." I waited a moment. "I . . . I can't be responsible. I don't want another school flute. Really, I don't."

That Friday we went on Christmas break. I walked out with Helena and she asked for the hundredth time that week if there was anything wrong with me.

"No," I said. "I told you about the flute. I told *everyone* about the flute. Even stupid Robert knows about the flute! I just want to go away from this school for the next two weeks and have everybody forget that I was ever in the Stage Orchestra at all." I set a marching pace down the hill and Helena kept up.

I stopped short out in front of Hose Company No. 6. "Look, I'm sorry," I told her. "I promise not to be such a grouch when we get back." I smiled and Helena smiled too. "It'll be a whole New Year. Everything will be different, right?"

"Right," she said.

"Merry Christmas, girls!" One of the firemen was dressed up in a red suit and white beard. He came out to the sidewalk waving and handed us each a little square box of seashell chocolates. I hesitated. It's a *gift*, I told myself.

I smiled. "Thank you!" I said. "My first gift this year!"

"Addie! Got a minute?" Elliot called from the doorway of the minimart.

"Sure," I said. I probably had all night if I wanted it. Mommers' car wasn't in front of the trailer and it was Friday—not a night she was likely to show up.

I went inside, where the smell of warm coffee greeted me. I took a deep breath through my nose. "Ahh . . . makes me wish I liked the stuff," I said. Soula laughed out loud. "Hey, look at what the fire guys up at Hose Six gave me." I held up the box of seashell chocolates. "Six pieces. Want one?"

"You keep those for later, Cookie. Make a cocoa

for yourself," she said. "And then see if you can manage opening up that box." She stuck her chin toward Elliot and he brought a wrapped box out from behind the counter and set it down. Soula batted her lined eyes at me.

"Oh, you're kidding. For me?"

Elliot nodded.

"Geez, I don't have anything for you yet."

"Open it!" Elliot said impatiently.

I read the card. "Merry Christmas, from a big bunch of numbskulls. Soula, Elliot and Rick." I laughed. Then I started picking at the tape.

"Oh no! You're one of *those*?" Elliot huffed. "You have to rip into it, girl!" He came toward me.

"Back!" Soula warned, and she pointed a finger at him. "She knows how to open a Christmas package, thank you very much."

Elliot hissed at Soula and pretended to spaz over the agony of watching me. I went even slower just to tease him. Finally, I pulled out my second gift that holiday: a pair of seriously warm and water-proof boots—the comfortable sneaker type. The boots were filled with more presents. I got new socks, a bottle of kitten pink nail polish, hot cocoa mix and some microwave popping corn.

I tried on the boots. Elliot poked his thumb up and down on my toe. "Perfect fit, don't you think?"

"Perfect," I said. "Thank you so much."

We visited for an hour or so. I did a little sweeping up and then danced with the broom to the Christmas tunes that came over the radio. Elliot cranked up the volume for me. Later, I saw Mommers' car come past and stop at the trailer.

"I better go," I said. But before I left, Soula sneaked me another wrapped package.

"You can open this one back at your place," she whispered. "It's nothing exciting but it is a bit personal."

I thanked them again and headed home, my arms wrapped around the full boot box.

Mommers was already watching *Jeanette for the Judgment* when I got in. "You're home late," she said. Then, seeing my box, she added, "Oh God, what's that?"

"New boots and some other fun stuff," I said. I shot a glance in the direction of the minimart. "They're so nice. It's a good gift, don't you think?" I spread my presents out on the table.

"A little odd," she mumbled. "Ooh, chocolates!"

She noted the little square box.

"I have something else here too," I said. I opened the package from Soula and found six pairs of bikini underpants inside—all pastel colors. "Oh!" I laughed. "Good for Soula! Look, Mommers, she knew I wouldn't want to open these in front of Elliot."

"I think he *knows* you wear underpants," Mommers said. She smirked at me. I raised an eyebrow back.

"I'm gonna bake cookies for them tonight."

"Homework," Mommers said.

"School break!" I fired back.

"Oh yeah. I forgot. Ha! Look at this, Addie. Jeanette is on a roll. Pet ownership dispute. She colored her hair too, I think. Or maybe a henna."

"That's great," I said. "Hey, Mommers, why are you here tonight?"

She looked at me strangely. "I live here!" she said.

"Yeah, but it's Friday night."

"Pete had something else to do."

"Well, can I make the cookies?" I asked again. I opened the cupboard and checked on our baking supplies. No chocolate chips, but there was sugar, and flour, and baking soda and salt. We had four eggs left in the fridge and two sticks of butter.

"What kind?" Mommers asked.

"Sugar cookies," I said.

"What about dinner? Is there anything good?"

"Want an egg?"

"An egg?" She stopped to laugh at something Jeanette said. "Yeah, I'll have an egg. With toast?"

"Sure," I said.

So I scrambled up two of the eggs for our dinner. I used the tiniest bit of butter on our toast so there'd be enough for the cookies.

After *Jeanette*, Mommers signed on for a chat and I did my baking. I played the CD Hannah had lent me. I liked the stories the songs told. Mostly, they were about Irish people coming to America when times were hard. They hoped for such simple things, like meals and beds. I felt glad I had those things. They wanted a kitchen to cook in. Like this one, I thought as the timer rang to remind me to pull the cookies from the oven.

Over at the computer Mommers swore under her breath. "That is the dreariest music I think I've ever heard."

"No it's not. They're just . . . hoping," I said.

"They're whining." She sneered. I had to laugh at that just a little.

"Is that a flute?" she asked. "I do like that part."

I stopped to listen. "I think it's a fife or a recorder," I told her.

"Can you play that though? Can you play it on the flute?"

I turned my back on her. "No. Not anymore."

"What do you mean, not anymore?"

"I took myself out of music."

"What?"

"I quit." I turned around. "I . . . I took the flute back to Borden School."

Mommers just sat there with her mouth open for a few seconds. "Addie?"

"I had to," I said. "I should have returned that flute when we moved. I'm glad it's gone."

Mommers had snagged one of my seashell chocolates. I watched her holding it between her thumb and finger. "Hmm." She took a bite. "Can't they get you one at this school?"

"Yes, probably. But I don't want to play the flute anymore," I said.

Mommers put the chocolate into her mouth and

rolled it to one cheek. "I'm gonna do something about this, Addison," she said with her mouth full. "My kid needs a flute." She glanced at her computer screen and returned to her chat. She leaned forward to type something in. I didn't worry about Mommers borrowing another flute for me. I didn't have to.

I found a stump of white crayon and decorated three lunch bags with snowflakes. I was no artist but the white crayon looked good on the brown bags. I packaged the cookies for Soula, Elliot and Rick. I cut up the ribbon they had used on my gift and tied the tops shut. Just as I pulled the loops tight on the last bow, Mommers shut down the computer. She looked up and out of the clear blue said, "Give me the phone, will you? I'm gonna let Dwight take you between Christmas and New Year's."

Yes! Another Christmas gift!

waiting for normal

I felt bad that I was counting the days until Christmas. This year, I wanted Christmas Day to come . . . *and go.* On December 26 I'd be on the bus heading up to Lake George. I could not help thinking that I'd have my *real* Christmas there with Dwight and Hannah and the Littles—*all to home.* Mommers didn't seem to be into celebrating this year. On the twenty-third, we still didn't have a tree.

I trotted back from the Heads and Roses Laundry Stop with our plastic basket under one arm. The torn webbing poked into my side as I fiddled with the doorknob to the trailer. Mommers yanked it open for me. She was in her robe. She twirled a shower cap on one finger.

"Jeez, Addie! How many loads does that make?"

"Three," I said, setting the basket down hard on the table. I sighed.

"You can't wait to get out of here, can you?" She cocked her hip.

I didn't answer. I started to clear a space on the table so I could fold the clothes. We still had boxes of office supplies sitting around—more than before, in fact—and most of them unused. I made a stack, moved it to the living room and came back for more. I came across the little square box my seashell chocolates had come in. I had forgotten about them. My mouth watered. I tipped the box and the inner sleeve slid out. All but one of the shell-shaped hollows was empty. I dumped the last chocolate into my hand and turned it over once.

Mommers had a funny bite, and by that I mean a distinctive one. Her upper row of teeth was perfectly straight. But her bottom row had a single tooth that came considerably forward. That's what I was looking at: her bite mark on my last chocolate.

"Hey, Mommers, did you eat them all?" I asked, holding up the box.

"Huh? I don't know. I ate some, I guess."

"*All*," I said. "You ate *all*, except this." I held up the bitten piece.

"Pfft. Give me a break, Addie." She grabbed a towel from my clean laundry pile and shook out her hair. "I'm gonna take a long hot one," she said.

"If you had to bite it, you could have at least finished it!" I complained.

Mommers reached over, took the chocolate out of my fingers and popped it in her mouth. "Happy?" she said.

"Mommers!"

"Merry Christmas to me!" She laughed and had to catch the chocolate before it fell out of her mouth.

"You're not funny!" I said. She slammed the bathroom door, then poked her head back out.

"Why do you want to go up to Dwight's so bad anyway? What's so special? What are you chasing after?" she asked. I stood thinking about that just a little too long. Mommers slammed the door again and I heard her turn on the shower.

"I'm not *chasing* after anything," I mumbled to myself. "I'm *waiting*. Waiting for *normal*." I shook a paper bag open and started to pack for my trip.

jingle all the way

There was nothing normal about Christmas at the trailer. First, Mommers went out to see Pete—"just for a drink"—on Christmas Eve at about five o'clock. I didn't see her again until she came in at nine on Christmas morning.

"Merry, merry!" she piped. "Now, I just have to go in here a minute." She walked into her bedroom with her coat still on. Through the half-closed door, I heard her rummaging around in her closet. Then I heard the swish of wrapping paper and the snapping of tape.

I put hot water on for cocoa. "Did you have breakfast?" I called.

"I had a muffin at Pete's," she said.

"I guess I knew that," I mumbled.

"Huh? Did you say something?"

"No." I had the Christmas parade on the TV and I stood by the stove waiting for the water, waiting for Mommers and waiting for the float that carried the big guy in the red suit. That was it. I was having a *waiting* Christmas.

"Okay! Tah-dah!"

I turned to see Mommers holding a small stack of hastily wrapped gifts. I pushed a smile out. "I have something for you, too," I said.

"You first! You first!" Mommers shoved the presents toward me.

I opened a new sweater and stopped to admire it. She pushed the next package toward me. "Open it! Open it!" she squealed.

"Okay, okay! Jeez, can we slow down?" I pulled a new notebook and a pen full of lime green ink out of the wrappings.

"That's a new vocab book," Mommers said. "The other one must be full."

"Close," I said.

"Okay, okay. Here. Next one."

I froze, looking at her. "You're trying to get out of here, aren't you?" I said. "You haven't even taken off your coat."

"Addie! No." She looked away from me, then

back again. She took off the coat, let it drop to the floor.

"Then why are you hurrying me?"

"This is Christmas! It's exciting! Come on, Addie! Can you be excited?"

"I suppose I can," I said. The next gift was a box of seashell chocolates—bigger than the one the guys at Hose Company No. 6 had given me.

"I won't eat a single one," Mommers promised. She lit a cigarette and blew a ring into the air. "Now, where's my present?" She held out one hand and did a little wiggle.

"It's just something small," I said as I handed her the package.

"Ooh!" Mommers squealed as she tore into the wrapping. "My! What is this?" Her mouth was open in a happy grin.

"It's a paper shade," I said. "For the famous naked light bulb." I pointed up to the center of the kitchen where the bulb hung on its cord. "I got it at the Tibetan store up on Nott Street."

"Oh, good idea!" Mommers squealed. She held the shade up and flicked the little tassels with her fingers. "I've always hated that stinkin' bare bulb, that antique chicken warmer!" She cackled a laugh.

I grinned.

Mommers glanced at the TV. The Christmas parade had ended. She picked up the remote and jabbed at the buttons. "All church services and choirs today," Mommers growled. She deepened her voice and sang, "Holy! Holy! If only Dwight would spring for cable. Ha! That'll never happen. He's such a—" She made a rude noise. She picked up the remote again and aimed to kill.

"Leave it on. It's nice," I said. Truth was, the trailer felt cozy to me and listening to the choirs made it more Christmassy. (Mommers had decided to skip the tree altogether.)

She put on a solemn face and began mouthing the words along with the choir. She looked like she was yawning. She made her eyelids flutter wildly until she looked completely deranged.

"Mommers," I laughed. "Cut it out! Come on, what are we doing today?" I asked. "Can we make a big dinner together?"

"Well, actually . . ." Mommers went into the kitchen and threw open the cupboards. "I was going to check and see what there is for you."

"For *me*?"

"Uh-huh," she said, all casual like.

"You *are* leaving, aren't you?"

"Well, so are you!" Mommers put her hands on her hips. "You're going to Dwight's."

"I'm not going until tomorrow," I said. "I can't believe it. You're leaving on Christmas. Is that why you told Dwight not to bring Brynna and Katie down on Christmas Day? Because you weren't gonna be here?"

"No! Listen to you grilling me, Addie! Pete and I are going for a sleigh ride up in Saratoga today. You know, like 'jingle all the way'!" She pretended to hold the reins. When I didn't respond she sagged and came toward me. "Aw, Addie, he planned it special. What was I gonna say?"

"How about, 'I have a twelve-year-old daughter. Can she come too?'"

Mommers laughed. Then she stopped. "Addison, can't you just understand? The trouble with Pete is he's not a family guy. He doesn't get the whole kid thing." She paused. "But he will." A grin spread across her face. "Wanna know how I know?" I watched her make a frame with her hands—a sort of heart shape. She lowered her hands to her belly and stopped there. She hummed a single line of "Rock-a-bye Baby." "That's how," she whispered.

My hair prickled up all over my head. My neck went hot, then icy. "Oh, Mommers! No!" I said. I shook my head. "Oh, I'm sorry to be saying that to you. But Mommers, this can't be!"

"It is," she said flatly. She pulled her coat on and picked her gloves up off the table. "It's going to be great. We haven't had a baby around in so long."

"We don't need a baby!" I was yelling now. "You . . . you shouldn't have done this! You just said Pete is not a family guy. Who's gonna—"

"Mind your own business!" she hollered back. "I shouldn't have told you. And I do *not* want Dwight or *anyone* knowing *anything* about this," she warned. She grabbed my hat and tugged it onto her head. She jerked open the door and stepped outside. "Couldn't you have just supported me?"

I didn't answer.

Mommers huffed at me. "Oh, Merry stinkin' Christmas!"

Slam!

another thing to borrow

I got myself up the hill to catch the bus to Lake George. Mommers had come home very late and was still sleeping. I'd left a note reminding her to take care of Piccolo for me, but I had loaded the food and water dishes just in case. I put my face near the cage door and whispered, "Bye, Pic, you little cutie, you. I'll see you in a few days." Whiskers twitched back at me.

As the bus hummed up the Northway, I thought about Mommers and her baby. I wished she hadn't told me. Instead, I thought of how she'd left Katie and Brynna and me. I pictured a new baby alone and waiting somewhere. My heart spilled. I didn't care how much Mommers loved having babies. I couldn't be happy about this one. I just couldn't.

By the time I got off the bus in Lake George, I

was miserable. I even felt kind of sick, maybe from the ride. But Dwight and Hannah were there at the bus station, all smiles. I took in some fresh air and put on a grin. The Littles hopped up and down all over me like puppies. My paper bag suitcase tore open and we all had to carry my stuff to Hannah's car in our hands.

"Good thing about the gift," Brynna said slyly. "You know which one?" she said to everyone but me. Her eyes twinkled.

Katie chimed in. "Oh you mean the . . . the . . ."

"Shhhh! Don't tell, Katie!"

"It's a purprise for you, Oddie," Katie said, nodding at me.

"She means surprise," Brynna told me.

"That's right," Dwight said. "We did do that one right, I guess." He winked at Hannah.

They had waited Christmas for me. I mean they had *really* waited Christmas. Everyone's presents were still wrapped under the tree.

"We only goed through stockings," Katie said earnestly. "Be-cept yours, Oddie. We didn't goed through yours." She shook her head. "'Cause that's yours." I laughed. I had almost forgotten how funny she was.

"You guys are the best!" I said. "And look at how pretty everything is!"

Paper snowflakes dangled on nearly invisible threads through the entire room. There must have been fifty of them. I smelled chicken—I was pretty sure—roasting in the oven, and the doorways were decorated with pine boughs.

"Blow! Blow!" Katie waved a magazine in the air and the flakes swayed.

"Pretty cool," I said.

There were changes to the kitchen area—one wall of real cupboards, which, Dwight and Hannah explained through giggles, was the most romantic thing they could come up with to give each other for Christmas.

"We're pitiful!" Hannah said, leaning on Dwight.

It's finally Christmas, I thought.

Katie dove under the tree and brought out a present and handed it to me.

"I'm first?" I asked.

"Yeah. Because you need it. You really, really need it," said Brynna with a grin.

"Help me out, then, you guys! Come on!" We tore open my gift—a totally sporty-looking duffel bag—electric blue with black straps.

"Oh, perfect!" I laughed now that I knew their joke.

Brynna ran to get my loose clothes and started to put them in the bag. I watched her making decisions about where everything fit best. My jeans folded in thirds on the bottom of the bag. My new bikini unders rolled and tucked into the side pocket. Fresh Whisper and my hairbrush went perfectly into the end pocket. She took her time and worked seriously. I got it into my head that that had something to do with her having the Love of Learning.

"That's nice, Brynna," I said. "Thanks."

After all the presents were opened, and after we ate our chicken dinner, Dwight and I washed dishes together.

"Brynna's really smart, isn't she?" I said.

"Sure, I guess she is. Why do you say so?" Dwight's voice was soft and interested.

"I just see it." I shrugged. "It's little things. Like how she knows all the numbers in Hannah's cataloging system downstairs, and even the way she just packed my new duffel."

"Hmm." Dwight thought for a second. "She

likes to control things." He grinned. Then he scrunched his brow. "She's having a hard time, you know. We talked to a counselor about it." I was surprised but I kept listening. "It's confusing for her to be away from your mom. She remembers more than Katie does. You know what I mean?" He handed me a plate and I rinsed it. "And I don't think she's as resilient as you."

"Resilient?"

"Yeah . . . bounce-backish," Dwight said, then he laughed at his own definition. I made a mental note to put that one in my new vocab book. It'd make a good first entry.

"I guess I do bounce," I said. "But see, that's what I mean, Brynna is always thinking," I said. "She's so . . . so . . ."

"Meticulous?" Dwight offered. (Another one for Webster's.) "You're right. She is." He nodded and squeezed suds off the sponge onto the dishes in the sink.

"But it seems like it hurts her. Maybe I bounce because I'm like that 'no brain, no pain' thing. Like if I was smarter . . ." I was suddenly aware that Dwight had stopped still and was staring at me.

"Ya know, Addie . . . there's nothing wrong with

you, hon. You're very smart. You know that, don't you?"

I shook my head. "No. School stuff is really hard for me. You remember."

"You bet I do. I went to all your school conferences. You have dyslexia."

"There's a name for it? Dis-what?"

"Dyslexia. It's a learning disability."

"My spatial relationship stuff? The reading and writing?"

"Yes. That's part of it. But it's all about *how* you learn, not how smart you are. You have to work harder and you have to work differently. But you do it. You make good grades and you play the . . ."

I didn't let him say it. "I think the teachers just get me through everything," I said. "They just . . . *give* me the better grade or something."

"Who says?" Dwight looked all flustered. He turned from the sink to face me. "That's what teaching is: getting kids through. What's this about? Is this stuff coming from Mommers?"

Mommers.

Looking into Dwight's eyes, I wanted to tell him about the boyfriend and the overnights and the baby. But in a split second I decided not to.

Eventually, I was going to have to go home. Being at the inn was just a vacation, a party. In my real life, Mommers was all I really had.

"Addie, you okay?"

I blinked at him and swallowed. "Mommers just knows I didn't get the Love of Learning."

"Love of learning? What, and she did?" Dwight laughed. "I'm sorry. I didn't mean that," he said. He straightened up like he was making himself behave. "Addie, I'd say you have the love of learning as much as anybody does. Don't let anyone tell you you aren't smart enough or good enough? Okay?"

"Okay," I said.

I don't think it was that conversation with Dwight, and it wasn't anything in particular that happened while I was there, but while I was at the inn I started feeling like a Tootsie Roll Pop. On the outside I was having a shiny-good colorful time. But I could feel my chewy, gooey center squishing and squashing inside of me.

Each day we did fun things: We went sledding on the hill in front of the inn. We built snowmen and gave them radish mouths and carrot noses. We listened to music and danced in the big, unfinished great room of the inn, where the new stone fire-place roared with its first blaze. I hung on to Dwight's strong hand as he swung me around and around to the music, then sent me sliding across the new floor on my socks. I read a hundred books a day to Katie while Brynna mouthed all the words, which she had memorized. I sat in an old soft chair at night and braided Hannah's hair while she sat on the floor between my feet. But I always felt weird—sad—at the end of every day. And all too quickly, we were out of days.

The last night, we set the table together. I watched Katie folding napkins and Brynna marching in with the silverware. Hannah swished by in her oven mitts with the casserole dish and Dwight struck a match to light the candles. I froze the picture. This was the end. It'd all been mine but only for a while. I had borrowed it—like the flute—and tomorrow I'd have to return it. I knew then and there that I couldn't keep on doing it forever. Something had to change.

loads of snow

In January we had storms that spat down snow
two and three feet at a time. At school we joked
that we'd been closed every other day. But the
Empty Acre never looked as good as it did wearing
a fresh blanket of white. Good until the city started
dumping truckload after truckload of secondhand
snow there. They said the streets had become dan-
gerously narrow. The banks were too high to see
around. So for several days all of us on the corner
of Freeman's Bridge and Nott listened to the
trucks come and go as they made use of the Empty
Acre.

I don't think any of us would have minded the
big change of scenery except that one day they
poured a truckload of the dirty stuff practically on
top of Soula's home. I was coming back from the

215

Heads and Roses with our busted laundry basket stabbing my hip when I heard Elliot hollering. He was outside in his shirtsleeves.

"Can't you fill up the west corner first?" he wanted to know. "Come on, pal, you dumped that load practically *on* my friend's home!" He threw his arms wide. "She's got enough trouble! Can't you leave her a little sunlight?" The trucker just waved a hand at Elliot and shrugged. He started to pull away but Elliot stopped him. "Come on," he said over the noise of the truck's engine. "At least cut her a hole." But the driver indicated that he didn't have a plow on the front.

"Sorry, I just do what I'm told and collect my paycheck," he called over the rattle of the engine. He pulled out onto Nott Street and headed away— probably to get more snow.

I heard Elliot curse. He picked up snow in his bare hands, packed it and flung it at the mound the truck had left. That's when I set my basket down on the step of the trailer and went across the street.

"Hey, Elliot!"

"Oh, hi, Addie."

"What's up?" I said.

"Eh." He shrugged. "I'm cooling down, you

216

could say." He let out a little laugh.

"How bad is it from the inside? The snow pile, I mean."

"Big dirty hill. Right in front of her windows," he said grimly.

We went inside together and made our way through to the Greenhouse. Looking out the window, I could see he was right. Soula was sitting in the papasan chair with a mug of chocolate. She smiled at me and winked.

"Did you have to pry him off the front of the truck?" she asked. She gestured toward Elliot with her chin. "He's very *pit bull*, don't you think?"

"Oh, cute." Elliot nodded at her. "I was trying to look out for you," he said.

"My hero," said Soula. "But you can't fight the city, Elliot. Lookie here, I got me something I've never had before." She swept a hand toward the window and the mound of snow beyond. "Welcome to *my* avalanche!"

I laughed.

Elliot said, "Oh, play it, Pollyanna! Like everybody wishes they had one of those in the yard!"

"What do you know?" Soula teased. "You jealous? It's mine but you want it, don't you, Elliot?"

He rolled his eyes, let his mouth drop open.

"Maybe you could sell it," I joked.

"Don't you start too." Elliot wagged a finger at me. "Just wait until it melts! See who wants your avalanche then!"

"Well, we could play a joke," I said. "Let's offer it. Let's at least put a sign on it. It'll be funny."

So Elliot cut a panel out of a cardboard box and nailed it to a yardstick. Soula gave me one of her bright pink lipsticks and I wrote AVALANCHE FOR SALE in big letters. Then I went outside, climbed the mound and planted our sign in the snow.

You'd think upstate New York would be better prepared for winter weather, but I'd been there all my life and it seemed like snow always brought things to a standstill, at least for a while. There wasn't much to do on a day off from school except walk back and forth from the trailer to the mini-mart, which I did plenty. Every fresh snowfall, I walked out and made a set of footprints. Then I always stepped in them again on my way back.

The plow came to our lot irregularly—sometimes Mr. Rose showed up with a snowblower and he cleared the parking spots in front of the Laundromat. But the patch out in front of the trailer was never completely free of snow. I told Soula and Elliot that that was why Mommers didn't park her car there much anymore—it was too likely to get stuck. I worried sometimes that I was bothering them by coming over so much, so I asked them one day if it was all right.

"Why do you think we gave you the boots?" Soula chuckled. I figured I had better go along with that, especially if I wanted somewhere to hang out.

I discovered a new sport that same day—*cardboarding*. This was sliding down Soula's avalanche while standing on a sheet of cardboard from a box at the minimart. Elliot swore it was going to become the next new event for the Winter Olympics and he considered himself my sled maker—said he was skilled with a utility knife. Soula sat inside the Greenhouse watching every run I took, while Elliot ran back and forth from the window to the store.

"The inconvenience of customers!" he yelled through the glass. "I'm missing the grace and loveliness of the Addison Schmeeter on Ice and Snow Show!"

"Grace! Yeah, right!" I laughed. "It's the outfit, isn't it?" I said, looking down at my too-short snow pants. I took a few Frankenstein steps toward them, rolled my eyes and pressed my nose on the glass.

"They wear knickers in the Alps!" Soula called back to me. "You're lookin' fine, Cookie!" She pointed upward to send me on another climb.

They made up cards with numbers on them and gave me scores. Elliot scored me highest for wicked falls—tens, if I went heels over head.

"Are you trying to kill me?" I asked at the glass.

Soula liked graceful finishes, so even when I had to pull my face out of the snow, I put my arms up over my head in a V for victory.

"That's right, Little Cookie! Stick those landings!" she called. We laughed so hard I was afraid I'd pee in my snow pants. But it would have been worth it just to see Soula doubling over with giggles the way she did.

Finally, the sun dipped behind the old Big N building and I started to get cold. I went in and drank a hot chocolate while my mittens dried on the radiator inside the Greenhouse.

"How about you go tell Elliot to bring a chicken

pot pie back here," Soula said. "Let's eat together tonight, huh, Cookie? Think it's all right with your momma?"

"I'm sure it is," I said.

I found out that night that not too many things smell as good as a chicken pot pie when it's cooking. I also found out it needs a long, long time in the oven. I guess Soula didn't know that either; she fell asleep before it was done.

Sometimes I sat alone in the trailer. I did homework. (School didn't stay closed forever.) Then I watched TV, and I let Piccolo take fun runs up in my bunk. I listened to Hannah's CD of Irish songs or just let the radio play. I had a project too: keeping track of what was in the kitchen cupboards.

I had two boxes of mac and cheese, almost half a box of Cheerios, a sleeve of saltine crackers, a bag of egg noodles and a box of brownie mix. In the can department, I had two tomato soups, one fruit cocktail, and one cheapy tuna—the squishy, cat food kind. There were two eggs in the fridge, along with four carrots, half a quart of milk and almost half a jar of peanut butter. There were three hamburger buns in the freezer. It didn't look like much but I had things figured out. Each box of mac and cheese would make two meals. Each can of tomato soup was ten and three quarters ounces of pure possibility. I could mix it with the cooked egg noodles and cat tuna. I could pour it over a toasted hamburger bun. Or, I could just make soup like the label on the can said. But whatever I did, I had to be careful about the groceries. Mommers had been gone for six nights in a row.

She had called the first night and said it was all because of the snow that she couldn't get home. Getting through the city was hard just after a big snowfall. But she could have come home between some of those storms if she'd wanted to, and I guess I knew that.

Still, snow wasn't a *bad* excuse and that's exactly the one I used when Dwight called to find out when I'd like to come visit again.

"Oh, gosh," I said. "With all this snow, you know, I don't think the buses are even picking up at Nott Street right now. It's a mess. You should see the banks—higher than my hat. You got a lot of snow too, don't you?"

"Uh . . . yeah, it's been a challenge. The truck isn't running right or I'd have been down to check on the trailer by now." I waited. "Addie, you said no buses. How can that be?" Dwight asked. I could almost see him scratching his head.

"Oh, the banks get tall," I said.

"No, I mean how can the buses just stop completely? Addie, I'm sure you're wrong about that. Have you checked since the last storm? Want me to call the bus company?"

"No," I said. I fought to keep my voice easy. "I'll look into it."

"Do it soon, hon. We want to see you."

"Okay," I said.

"Can I talk to Denise? She home?"

I thought for a second. "Hey, Dwight? Dwight?" I spoke loudly. "I think maybe we're losing our connection."

"I'm here. Can you hear me?" he asked.

"Dwight? Did you say something? Well, I guess I'm gonna hang up now. Bye, Dwight. If you can hear me, bye!" I set the receiver back in the cradle and stood staring at it. My eyes burned with tears and the phone went blurry. "Don't ring, don't ring," I whispered.

It rang. I let it ring and ring and ring.

a visit from grandio

I poured water into the poinsettia plant Dwight had given us. I watched Mommers' cigarette butts float up and sink down again in the pot. The plant was still gorgeous. I knew I should clean the butts out, but I didn't want to touch them.

From the corner of my eye, I caught a flash of blue at the picture window. I went closer and watched Mommers stepping over the snow and into the footprints I had made in previous days. She burst in through the door.

"Those people are getting weirder and weirder." She pointed toward the minimart with her thumb. "Now they're trying to sell snow in winter!"

"Oh, the avalanche? It's a joke. I did that," I told her. "And it's been there for days."

"Yeah, so what's your point?"

"You've been *gone* for days," I said.

"Oh, don't give me that!" Mommers glanced around the inside of the trailer. She turned her palms up. "Anything fall off this tin can while I was gone? Did the pipes burst? Did you run out of food?"

"No," I said.

"Well okay then!" She pushed at her hair and started going through the mail. "Did Dwight's check come?"

"Yeah, it's there. It's early."

"Where?" She seemed annoyed. I reached and slid the envelope out of the pile of junk mail. I pushed it toward her. "Oh, good!" she sighed. She tore it open.

"We need to go grocery shopping," I said. "We're out of *everything*. And Piccolo needs food. I've been giving her cereal and carrots. Her poop is getting messy."

"Make a list," she answered, flapping a hand at me. "But only what you *really* need."

"What's that mean?"

"Well . . ." she said, her voice high and too cute for comfort. "We're in a little pinch. It's just temporary. We'll catch up."

225

"Mommers . . ."

"Pete just got a little mad about the last credit card bill. I worked it out with him but we're a little short on cash."

"How short?"

"Mind your business, Addison." She looked closely at Dwight's check for the first time. There was a second of silence, then she started to swear. She banged the table with her fist.

"What!" I said. "What's wrong?"

"He postdated it! I can't cash it until the first!"

"But that's when he usually sends it," I said.

"Yeah, but if he's going to send it, why not just date it early? I can't cash it until . . . when?" She looked at the calendar. "Thursday!" She slammed the table again. "Dwight loves this! He loves it when things don't go right for me! It's not enough he took my babies, he's gotta mess up my entire life! What am I gonna tell Pete?" She covered her face with her hands.

While Mommers was away, it was easy to be mad at her. But now that she was home and upset and crying, I felt bad for her again. Her hair was in tangles and she was smearing her mascara.

Then I reminded myself, *She always does this.*

"Addie, Addie." She sniffed and started to smile again. "You could ask your big friend at the mini-mart to cash this check. She could just hold on to it until Thursday." Mommers wore a sell-it-to-me grin.

"Uh . . . I don't know," I said. I didn't want Soula to know that Mommers had money problems.

"Addie." Mommers leaned toward me. "Don't you want to eat? What about the little fur ball over there?" She pointed to Pic's cage. "And what about me? Come on. What's important?"

"Fine. I'll ask her."

"Okay. Go now! Go, go, go! Here. Take the check and show it to her. Tell her Dwight is good for it. His checks never bounce. If she says yes, come back and I'll sign it over to her."

Of course Soula agreed. Mommers signed the check over to the minimart and we got our cash. But I wondered how long it'd be before there would be more problems. As it was, she only came home with half the stuff on my grocery list.

Still, it was a good thing we had some food in the house because when the weekend came, Grandio stopped by. Mommers would have

227

screamed him off the front step if she'd been home, but she wasn't.

"Dwight asked me to check in," Grandio said in that gravelly voice of his. He pushed his way inside. "He'd be here himself if the truck was running. The babies have fevers and he didn't wanna leave Hannah without a car. Everything okay?" He glanced around.

"Brynna and Katie are sick?"

"Just the flu. Phone working?" He lifted the receiver and put it to his ear.

"Yep. Things are great." I smiled but he didn't look at me.

"Well, what's the deal with the answering machine? Dwight says he's leaving messages but you and your mother don't call back." He looked at me sternly. I shrugged, held my breath. Grandio looked in the fridge, opened a cupboard and poked a few of the cans and boxes with his thick finger. "Well, you need anything, girl?"

"No sir," I said.

"All right, then. I'll call Dwight and let him know everything is all right."

"Thanks for stopping, Grandio." I watched him get back into his car. He gunned it too hard and spun out on the icy snow patches. I put on my coat and went out to give him a push. (I'd pushed Mommers out that same morning.) Grandio waved me off.

"I got it, I got it! Go back inside!"

"If you say so," I mumbled, and I did what he said. I listened at the door as he rocked the car and spun the wheels. I sighed. Dwight always said Grandio just liked doing things for himself. Mommers said he was a controlling old poop. I guess they were both right. I listened to his tires singing for another minute. Then he was gone. I heard myself breathe.

"Gone for now," I told Piccolo. "But you and me, pal, we're on notice." I knew Dwight would send Grandio by again if he didn't just show up himself.

valentine hearts

On Valentine's Day, I walked out of school with Helena and found Dwight out front. He was leaning on the truck. He grinned when he saw me and stood up.

"Shoot," I muttered. "That's my stepfather." I had not told Helena much about my family situation—just that I had decided not to spend time up in Lake George anymore.

"Oh, I guess he came to you this time," Helena said.

"Guess so," I answered.

"Do you want me to stay while you talk to him?" she offered. That creeped me out a little—like somehow I'd given her the idea that Dwight was some kind of dangerous weirdo that I shouldn't be alone with.

"No," I said. "It's fine. I'll see you tomorrow."

Helena walked away down Nott and I watched her go for a second before I went to Dwight.

"Hey!" he called.

"Hi," I said.

He pulled a pair of rumpled, construction paper valentines out from under the flap of his jacket. "A pair of cupids sent me," he said. "These are from the Littles."

I didn't answer.

"Oh, and I got you something." He took an entire roll of lunch tickets from his pocket and handed them to me.

"What did you do? Go inside the school to buy these?"

"Yeah," he said. "And I talked to your principal for a minute."

"Why? Everything is fine." I wrinkled my nose. It seemed funny to think of him being involved in my school stuff now, even though there was a time when he'd been a part of every parent-teacher conference.

"I just wondered if they had any concerns."

"Did they? I mean I'm sure Mommers would know if they did."

"No. They're crazy about you. Far as they can tell me anyway," he said. He paused, drummed his fingers on the side of the truck. "Of course, they wouldn't discuss much since . . . well, you know. Anyway, did you want to tell me about the flute?"

I shifted my feet. "You couldn't have done anything about it." I shrugged. "I just wanted to take care of it. It's over with. I'm glad."

He nodded; he didn't seem surprised to hear me say that. "What if we take a walk? One block over to Union Street. Got time?"

I sighed a big complaining sigh. "I guess so."

On the way Dwight held out a little plastic card. "This is a bank card. I want to show you how to use it in case you ever need money," he said.

"I won't ever need it," I said. But he pressed the card at me anyway.

"Twelve, six, three," he said. "It's easy to remember: Your age, then Brynna's, then Katie's." I almost laughed because it seemed as if he'd forgotten that we'd eventually get older. We walked up to the money machine at the Union Street Bank. Using the card was pretty easy; the machine told me what to do. "I keep a couple of hundred dollars in this account," he explained. "But it's probably safest if you just take twenty or forty at a time, okay? And never use the machine at night. Daylight only. It's safer."

"Okay," I said. "But I won't need it." He ignored me.

"This is the hardest part," he said. He drew his hand across his chin. "I need to do something wrong to do something right. Can you understand that?"

"I don't know what you're talking about," I said.

"I'm asking you to keep the card a secret. Don't tell Mommers and absolutely do not give her the code. This is for you, and it's for emergencies."

"Fine," I said.

"Good." Dwight smiled. "So how about an ice cream sundae while we get caught up a little?"

I shook my head no. I set my jaw so it wouldn't quiver.

Go home, Dwight.

"You've got a school vacation week coming up. Think the buses are running? Think Mommers will let you come up? I'll even come get you." I didn't answer. I toed a chunk of ice that had frozen to the sidewalk.

"Okay, Addie. What's going on here? Why don't you want to come up?" he said. I kicked harder and the ice broke loose and went sliding away like a hockey puck.

"It isn't *not wanting to*," I said.

"Well, then what? I don't get it. Wasn't Christmas good? Did I miss something?" Talk about missing something. I missed them so badly I could hardly stand it.

"No. Nobody did anything wrong," I said. I took a deep breath and the cool air burned inside my chest. "I just can't keep going up there and do all this . . . this *good-timey* stuff. It's not for real. You're right. Christmas *seemed* good. It did."

He thought for a moment. I avoided eye contact.

"But then it was over and coming home felt bad?" he asked.

I couldn't answer.

"Brynna and Katie keep asking for you. They need to see you. And I think you need to see them, too."

"I can just talk to them on the phone," I said.

"No. Not enough," he said flatly. "We're your family."

"Depends on how you look at it," I said, knowing I sounded snotty. Dwight grabbed my coat at the shoulders and tried to get his face right in my face.

"Hey! What's this all about?" he whispered. His eyes pinked up and I looked away.

"Nothing," I choked. "I just can't . . . pretend stuff anymore." I shook my head. "I'm too old to pretend stuff. I'm not . . . I'm not . . . *resilient*, Dwight. I'm really not."

"Oh, Addie." Dwight let go of my coat and reached to hug me, but I backed up fast and shook my head harder.

"No, don't!" I squeaked.

"Okay, okay," he whispered.

There was a long silence between us. Well, not true silence—the city kept happening around us. People passed us. The traffic moved up Union Street. I pulled terrible, skipping breaths into my chest and I wondered if anyone noticed us standing there. Did they wonder why a man and a girl would seem to be having a disagreement right on the street? Dwight covered his mouth with his hand, drew his fingers along his chin and kept sighing through his nose.

"Don't you have to get back?" I finally said.

"Don't forget, it's Valentine's Day."

He nodded slowly. "I guess so. But, Addie, we're not done with this."

"Well, I think we are. We have to be," I mumbled. I turned and headed down Union. Dwight followed behind me. When we got to the truck he gave me a ride to the trailer. He didn't come inside—thank goodness—just went around back to check on the electrical hookup. I followed him as much to keep him out of the trailer as anything. He said it was good to keep the snow cleared around the connection. I said I'd tell Mommers. Then I said good-bye to him. No hug. That was awful. But it was the right thing to do now.

Inside the trailer, I slipped Dwight's bank card into one pocket of my electric blue duffel bag. I rolled the duffel up small as I could and stuffed it into the back of my closet.

"Perfect, huh, Piccolo? Two things I won't be using so they might as well be in the same place." I thought about how Dwight had given me the lunch tickets, how he'd come all the way down to Schenectady to make sure I was all right. I thought about how mean I'd been. I looked at Pic again and said, "But I *had* to be mean."

I flopped on my back in my bunk. I put my feet up in the air and stretched my toes up till they reached the ceiling. In my mind I kept seeing the inn, my little sisters on the snowy hill, Hannah throwing her braid back as she stood in the doorway and Dwight strapping on his tool belt for work in the morning. I saw a table spread for dinner— "*Their* table. Not mine," I said. I pushed back tears. "Okay, now, I am not going to become some weenie-headed crybaby over this." I gently drummed on Pic's cage with my finger. "Ya get it, Pic?" I wiped my nose on my sleeve. "Besides, we'll be fine. We have a home and Mommers always makes it back before the food runs out."

I went into the kitchen and did another cupboard check even though I already knew exactly what was there. I called it out loud for Piccolo. "One box of mac and cheese, one brownie mix, one bag of goldfish crackers. One empty Cheerios box." (I'd kept it in there just for show.) I moved on to the cans. "Two tomato soups, one chicken noodle." I opened the refrigerator. "One stick of butter, one can diet soda, one jar pickles. And now for the Hamster Pantry." I turned and went to my closet. "Half a bag of seed and an almost full box of alfalfa blend. Well, Pic, given the size of me and the size of you, if food is wealth, you're the queen today," I said. "But if Grandio comes back, we're both in trouble." I remembered how he had poked at the boxes of food with his finger.

"That empty Cheerios box is a problem." I said, hopping off the bunk. I took the box down, and after rummaging around the trailer, finally stuffed it with a rolled-up magazine. The magazine filled the box and made it look full of cereal again. That gave me another idea. I checked the paper trash. I found two flattened mac and cheese boxes and put them back together with a glue stick from Mommers' office supplies. Then I filled the boxes full of plastic pushpins that she had never even opened. I shook the boxes.

"Hey, hey, hey, Piccolo! How do you like that? Sounds like real macaronis to me!" I shook again and danced a little cha-cha. I suddenly felt better than I had all day. I pulled the rumpled valentines from my sisters out of my jacket pocket. I smoothed them out and just stared at them for a minute. They were sweet, good decorations so I taped them to the paper shade I'd given to

Mommers for Christmas. Then I cut a chain of hearts from an old newspaper and hung those up, too.

I heated a can of tomato soup for my Valentine's supper and floated a little pat of butter on the top of it for good looks and richer taste. (Elliot taught me that.) I poured a little bit of Piccolo's seed right onto my bedcover. I let her come out and sit next to me. I sipped my soup and Piccolo filled her cheeks until her face looked like a puffy valentine heart.

the goosh in my gut

All my worrying about the February vacation snag was for nothing. Mommers happened to be home the night Dwight called and she flat out refused to let him have me. Of course, she did that just to rip Dwight but I was relieved that there wasn't a fight over it. I wondered if that meant that Dwight wouldn't ask again. I ignored the goosh in my gut. Mommers and I put away the groceries together. I counted meals as we worked.

One jar of applesauce goes with two cans of baked beans and makes four meals. One loaf of bread is eighteen slices including the heels—

"Hey! You must be mooching off your friends at the chubby-mart." Mommers elbowed me and giggled. "There's still a lot of macaronis in here." She shook the box.

"Not really," I said. "They're fakes. I just did it to make the cupboards look full. In case Grandio comes by again."

"Jack? Jack was here? Inside? He's got *no* business coming through *my* place!" Mommers insisted. "You can tell him no. You know that?"

"Mommers, it was Grandio, not some ax murderer."

"What did he want with us anyway?" Mommers asked.

"Well, Dwight sent him because he was worried about us."

"Yeah, right. Dwight's so worried he put us in this dump in the first place. If he's got a guilty conscience, it's because he deserves one!" Mommers simmered on and on. Finally, she sat down with a diet soda and lit a cigarette.

"Isn't that bad for your baby?" I asked.

"What? The baby *you* don't think I should be having?"

I shrugged. She took a puff.

"I'm gonna quit. I'm just . . . nervous right now."

"Are you staying?" I asked.

"I'm here tonight," she said. "Can you make

something for dinner? My feet are killing me." She thunked one foot then the other up onto a chair and sighed cigarette smoke out her nose. "I forgot how much being pregnant takes it outta me."

"Sure," I said. "I'll get dinner."

fiesta night

$\mathbf{S}$oula had been having energy problems. Her skin seemed kind of yellowy to me. She kept trying to powder up her face, but the yellow always showed through. I wondered if she'd ever had that last chemo treatment.

We had started to eat together most nights. When Soula let me cook for her, I felt good—like I was repaying some of her kindness. It turned out that she *liked* toast dinners. She said they reminded her of the food she had eaten as a kid.

"Makes me remember being young again," she told me one night as she took a bite of my special tomato soup on toast. "And there's not much on this planet that does that for this old girl anymore. You're my hero, Cookie."

Sometimes Elliot stayed around for dinner and

he and Soula got into salad wars. Elliot made the salad and Soula refused to eat it.

"The darker the greens the higher the vitamin C," he said. He slid the bowl under her nose and she swatted at him.

"Get that away from me, you fool!" she said. She turned her head away. "My ancestors didn't fight their way to the top of the food chain to look down and see me eating leaves!"

"Oh come on, Crab Cake. Afraid you might get healthy?" He shook the salad tongs at her.

"Look at me, Elliot!" Soula snapped. "Do I look like I'm about to get healthy?"

"Maybe you should try!" he shouted back.

I kept eating through their fight and wondering if everything would be okay. Poor Elliot. His face was red for half an hour. He didn't eat much—just pushed the food around on his plate. I made sure I ate lots of salad.

Later he brought Soula a Twinkies cake from out front and said he was sorry. "You should eat whatever you want," he said. Soula eyed him for a moment.

"Are you still gonna have that party for me after the last chemo?" She tapped a slipper-covered foot out in front of her and stuck out her bottom lip.

"Of course," Elliot told her.

"With a chocolate cake as big as a boulder?" she pleaded.

"Oh, that's disgusting," he said. Then he grinned at me and rolled his eyes.

A folded corn tortilla sizzled in the pan on the back of the stove and an oily haze hung in the trailer. I smelled meat and beans with chili powder.

"Hope you're hungry!" Mommers whooped as I walked in the door.

"I already ate tonight," I said. "I didn't think you'd be here."

"Well"—she grinned and brought her hands together in a loud clap—"you're gonna eat again! It's Fiesta Night!" She made big, sweeping loops in the air with one finger. She turned the tortilla with a fork, picked up a knife and split a green pepper in two. A mound of chopped onions and another of grated cheese were piled in bowls near her elbow. "Stir that pot of slop, will you?"

"What's the occasion?" I asked. I pushed a spoon into the meat and beans and stirred.

"Who needs an occasion? It's a fiesta!" she

repeated. I banged the spoon on the side of the pot to clean it. "You can't have too many leftovers," Mommers went on.

Well, she was right about that, I thought, as I twirled the spoon in my fingers. The refrigerator would be full of this stuff until—well, until she came back again. *All or nothing.* That was Mommers.

"Get me that head of iceberg from the fridge, huh?" she said. I did. When I handed it over, she put the blade of her knife up through the still-wrapped head of lettuce and stared at it for a second. She peeled back the plastic. "Oh! Oh! My long lost love!" she spoke to the pale green head. She puckered her lips and made loud kissing noises. "How could you stay away so long? I have waited"—kiss—"and waited for your return!" Kiss! Kiss! She went on and on. I don't know why I didn't laugh. It was funny enough. Instead, I picked up a sponge.

"Addie, you poop." Mommers dropped her lettuce puppet on the table. "What's the matter with you?"

I shook my head.

"What?"

"You," I said. I stood at the sink turning the faucet off and on over the sponge for no reason. "I know what you're doing," I said. "You're *trailer stuffing*."

"Trailer stuffing?"

"You're filling the place up with food." I swiped at the counter with the sponge. "You're gonna leave again."

Mommers froze for a second. "Well, I can't be here all the time! I have a job, ya know? Are you really mad at me? I can't believe this!"

"You're gone *all* the time," I said. I mashed the meat tray into the garbage and pushed it down hard twice. "We're gonna get caught again," I mumbled.

"Caught? No, no we are *not*." Mommers took a deep breath. "This isn't the same as . . . as before. Besides, you're *twelve* now! And look at you! Now listen, I'm here doing all this cooking and *you* are spoiling Fiesta Night, Addison. Come on. Get happy!" She went on chopping and frying. Then, without looking at me, she said, "And when I'm not here, you just . . . just . . . take *real* good care of yourself. Give me a little more time. Everything will work out fine."

I waited a couple of seconds. "Did you tell Pete?"

"I'll tell him about the baby when he needs to know," she said flatly.

"I didn't mean that," I said. "I meant did you tell him about me?"

She didn't answer.

I managed to eat one taco. Mommers ate three. While she settled in front of the TV with a diet soda, I cleaned up the kitchen. It seemed to take forever. The oil had splattered and she had set the meat-and-bean spoon down on the counter in about a dozen different places. There were puddles of slop everywhere. The more I cleaned, the madder I got. Mommers sat glued to *Jeanette*. I began to think it was better when I had the trailer to myself. At least then I only had to clean up my own mess. I scraped the meat and beans into a plastic bowl and stored it in the fridge. I scrubbed the pan in the sink and dried my hands.

"Finally," I said. Then I turned and saw the tortilla pan at the back of the stove and the onion bowl that I had missed on the table. I let a little growl out between my teeth.

"Hey, I'll get the rest," Mommers called to me.

"Oh," I said. "Really? That'd be nice. I'm going to do my homework."

In the morning, I found Mommers asleep in front of the TV. She had not moved since the night before. She had not done the last of the dishes. I went to her and shook her by the shoulder. "Don't you have to be at work soon?" I asked. She grumbled and rolled away from me. "Mommers," I said again. "You were gonna finish the kitchen. Remember?"

I took my shower and left for school.

making changes

"Hi, Elliot," I said as I entered the minimart. My backpack caught on the closing door and pulled me backward.

Elliot laughed and raised a hand. "Hi, Addie."

I looked at the empty lawn chair. Soula was usually right there when I came in from school. "Where is she?" I asked.

"Napping. It's not a great day," Elliot said, curling his lip.

"Oh. Poor Soula," I said.

"Yeah, only don't let her catch you saying that," he warned me. He put his finger to his lips. "No pity parties."

"Right. Hey, Elliot?" I kept my voice low. "Isn't it time for the last chemo?"

"Past time." He nodded. "Way past. But they're

holding off. She needs a break."

"Oh, that's good!" I said. I grabbed the broom and started sweeping my way past the dairy case. "Soula probably wants a break. She told me the chemo is the cure but the cure is a killer."

"Guess that's true," said Elliot.

I hung around awhile. I unpacked a box of chips and filled the coffee cup dispenser. Elliot took inventory in the candy aisle, marking off an order form he had on a clipboard.

"What's this week's winner?" I asked.

"Hershey's plain," he replied. Same as usual. "Not much changes around here." He made a big sigh and ran his hand over his short hair. "Then again, maybe that's a good thing." I have to admit, I thought he was being a bit dramatic.

"Aw, come on, Elliot. It's just chocolate," I said. "Hey, let's change something. Let's change the radio station!"

He gave me a silly grin. I got up on a stool and turned the tuning dial until I got a country-and-western station. We pushed back a cardboard display for disposable cameras and made a dance floor. Elliot was so good at leading that he made *me,* the clod, look like a pro. When I sat out, exhausted and sweaty, he danced the broom instead and just as easily too. From my milk crate stage, I sang with a twang into my ice scraper microphone. "One minute yo're beatin' all the odds, and the next, they're beatin' you!"

Soula never showed that afternoon. I left her a note to say hello and told her I'd be by tomorrow in case she had missed me. I shouldered my backpack and headed out.

"Hey, kiddo," Elliot said. He laughed when I pretended to be squooshed in the closing door. "Thanks for hanging around."

"Sure!" I said. I squeezed out the door and made a big circular wave with my arm from the other side.

I hopped the river of water that came streaming across the road from Soula's melting avalanche. I sniffed the air. Five o'clock on the corner had a sort of gassy smell about it, what with everyone coming and going. Elliot would be anchored to the register soon with everyone fueling up. The air was warmer than it had been in months. March was here. Spring was coming. I wondered how long before the tar would bubble up in place of all the slush and melting snow. I remembered popping the bubbles with Katie and Brynna back in September. I caught a sorry breath in my chest, along with a cloud of exhaust from an eighteen-wheeler.

I coughed my way into the trailer and closed the door quickly.

"Whoa! You don't need any of that stink filling up your little lungs, Pic," I said. I checked the stove just like I had for four nights running. Mommers had still not been back, or if she had been, she still hadn't done her share of the Fiesta Night cleanup. The taco pan was still on the back of the stove and I left it there. I scrubbed the saucepan I'd made my chicken noodle soup in (I was sick of beans after four nights in a row) and the knife I spread peanut butter onto my toast with. I rinsed the suds from my bowl, glanced at the pan full of oil and thought about cleaning it.

"Nope," I said. "Not gonna." I wiped up all around it. Then I turned on the radio, found the station Elliot and I had had so much fun with and kicked back. "From now on, Pic, I clean up after me and you. I'm changing my life!" I threw my head back and howled with the music.

my fault

I woke up way before the alarm the next morning. I was sure I had heard Mommers come in, but when I checked her room it was empty. I looked at the clock. It was just a little after five. I had hours before I needed to leave for school. I dug into the cupboard and pulled out a packet of cocoa mix— the *last* packet.

"Well, Piccolo, I got me one last cocoa and plenty of time to drink it," I said, still enjoying a Western twang. I flicked on the burner to start my kettle and went in for a quick shower.

When I came padding out in my bare feet and bathrobe a few minutes later I heard a strange sound—a mix of crackle and wind. Not right. The air smelled like burned tacos. I whipped around to see a black haze rising from the fry pan on the stove. There was a loud pop and it burst into flames. I reached for the handle. Too hot! I dropped the pan. The flames spilled and leaped. I grabbed the fire extinguisher. What had Dwight said? I pulled the pin and aimed. A watery spray hit the fire.

No foam! There should be foam!

The flames climbed the back wall and crept along the ceiling overhead. I let the extinguisher drop.

I ran to my bunk, grabbed Piccolo's cage and opened the trailer door. I turned and saw the fire swallow the Tibetan paper shade and the valentine hearts. The bulb shattered and I slammed the door.

I must have set Pic's cage down. I really don't remember that part. And I don't know how a person has enough sense to get out of a burning trailer but not get away from it. I just know that I stood there on the step swearing and beating my palms on the metal door until they stung with pounding heat.

A big soft arm wrapped me around the chest. "Come away, Cookie," Soula breathed. "Hurry now! Hurry!" She dragged me off the steps. "Your momma's not home, is she?"

"No. Wait! Piccolo!" I screamed. "Where's Piccolo!"

"Right here!" Soula said. She held the cage up by the handle for me to see. "Come on, now!"

By the time we crossed Freeman's Bridge Road, Soula was leaning on me instead of pulling me. Pic's cage bumped against her big side as she heaved her heft into the parking lot.

"Oh, Soula!" I choked. I looked over my shoulder at the trailer. "It's my fault! I was so stupid!"

"No, no, Cookie. Are you hurt?" Soula asked.

I looked at my hands. My palms were red. "No," I said.

We heard breaking glass and turned to see flames in the front picture window. Seconds later, the glass in my bunk space blew out. The walls turned black and folded in. My little square window frame glowed, red hot.

I heard the sirens up on Nott Street. Hose No. 6, I thought. Soula was still heaving every breath into her chest. Her eyes were wide. She set the hamster cage down with a thunk in front of her and leaned on it. The wires bent under her weight. I had never seen her so far from the store, so far from a place to sit down.

"Soula! Wait here!" I yelled. I ran up ahead and went into the minimart. I dragged her lawn chair out to her. She fell into it.

"I'm sorry, Soula!" I squatted down beside her and patted her arm. "You okay, Soula?"

She said, "I just need a minute. It's good you're safe, Little Cookie. You and your little hamster are safe." She stopped to breathe, then said, "Elliot and his fancy dial phone. Thank goodness!" Soula let out a sigh. "All I had to do was punch that button the second I saw the smoke." She closed her eyes, leaned back and smiled. I stooped beside her, rested my chin on her big arm and watched the fire trucks come down the hill.

Two trucks pulled right up in front of the trailer. Another pulled into the Empty Acre right beside the minimart. Within seconds, the firemen tore the door off the trailer. Two guys went in with masks over their heads.

"There's no one inside!" I hollered.

"It's okay, Cookie. They've got to do their job," Soula told me.

"Oh, Soula, what if one of them gets hurt . . . and all 'cause of me?"

"Don't think about it, Cookie. They'll come out."

Soula was right. What a relief to see them both

appearing out of the smoke and giving an all-clear signal to the others.

It was weird to watch them let the place burn. I mean they turned the hoses on it and all, but they weren't fighting to *save* anything now. Not really. Then I remembered something. I jumped up.

"What is it, Cookie?" Soula called after me. I didn't answer. I ran through the river of water to get to the fire truck that'd parked beside the mini-mart.

"Hey!" I called up to the cab. I grabbed the chrome bar and pulled myself up to the window. "Hey! I gotta talk to you. Please!"

"We're on a call!" the fire guy said sternly.

"It's about the electrical connection! The trailer is hooked up to the Laundromat next door. You've got to make sure they pull it!"

The guy practically knocked me off the truck when he swung the door open. He hit the ground running in his big boots. He splashed across Freeman's Bridge Road and disappeared behind the trailer. In a minute he was standing there again smiling at me and giving me a double thumbs-up with his big gloves. I knew that'd be the best thing I'd see that day. The Heads and Roses had been spared.

"It was good you told us about the electrical connection to the other building. That was smart, kiddo." One of the fire guys gave my head a pat.

"Yeah, I'm a real genius," I mumbled. All I could think of was the taco pan and how many days I'd let it sit.

"Looks like it started in the kitchen," the fire-man said.

"It did. There was a pan of oil on the stove. I was trying to make cocoa. I must have turned the wrong burner up to high." I wondered if I could get arrested for that and end up in a reform school or something. But so far, nobody seemed particularly mad at me. I stuck a finger between the bars of Pic's cage and she took it in her paws and sniffed it.

Gosh, what trouble I must smell like today.

"You prevented a double disaster," the fireman added, glancing at the Heads and Roses again. Then he smiled as he looked up at the sky. "Ah. Here it comes. Rain's gonna help."

I blinked as the drops started to fall.

a hero in the fog

Elliot arrived and immediately handed out coffees to the firemen. He moved Soula and Piccolo inside. Me, I felt stuck. Everyone tried to get me to go in. They said I shouldn't be out there in my bathrobe with bare feet and bare legs (plus I was bare underneath that robe, too), but I really couldn't feel anything. I watched the fire guys tie and haul the smoking black carcass of the trailer farther away from the Heads and Roses. Elliot brought me a pair of Soula's slippers. One of the Hose 6 guys put a heavy rubber coat over me and a paramedic asked me to hold some ice between my hands—just for a little while. I thought I was going to sink into the ground.

Mr. and Mrs. Rose arrived to check on the Laundromat. Their plaid pajama legs stuck out below their winter coats. They cupped their hands over their noses as they looked at the charred remains of the trailer. The stink could've made the vomit rise in the toughest of stomachs.

The early customers who were always at the corner in the morning stopped to eye the scene. A few cars pulled into the minimart lot. One lady arrived in a gray car and sat there talking on her cell phone with a clipboard across her steering wheel. She looked up at me every once in a while but never at the dead trailer.

Can't you see there was a fire? I thought. I sighed into the raining sky.

Minutes later, Grandio pulled up in his white car and stopped with his tires right next to my toes. "Addie! Girl! You okay?" He shielded his brow from the rain.

I nodded. "How did you know? Who called you?" I said.

"I called him." The lady from the gray car stepped up next to us. "Addie, I'm Mrs. Casey. I'm from the Department of Youth and Family Services."

I whirled and looked into the minimart. Soula was seated in her chair at the front window. She caught my eye, then looked down into her lap.

"Addie," Mrs. Casey spoke again. "How long has your mother been away?"

I knew Soula had ratted me out. She knew Mommers had been gone too much and now the state knew too. And I had a Mrs. Casey on my case.

"Forever," I said. "She's been away forever."

I turned toward Grandio and sighed. I knew I'd be going home with my next of kin.

"Can you keep Pic for a while?" I set the cage next to Soula. "Grandio will put up a fuss and he's already upset." I gazed out the window.

"Of course I will, Cookie. You know I will." Soula started to cry. She fiddled with the bent section of Pic's cage. Tried to pop it back out again. "I'm sorry about . . ." She glanced toward Mrs. Casey's car. "I couldn't see what else to do, Cookie. Truth is, I should have called them long ago."

"I know," I mumbled. I should have hugged her, should have told her everything was okay. Instead I said, "Thanks for taking Piccolo. I'll see you soon." I ran out the door and got into Grandio's car.

I sat waiting for him while he talked to the fire guys. My hands still hurt from the heat or ice, I wasn't sure. I could smell smoke in my wet hair. My damp bathrobe started to feel cold on my skin and my insides were slush. *Poor Soula.* It wasn't enough she was sick. I'd put her in a bad position all those months. Now she felt terrible and I felt terrible.

Finally, Grandio got into the car. "Jaypers, girl. We're all fogged up! Why didn't you turn up the blower?" he said.

He cleared the windshield with his hand and put the car in gear. We rolled slowly forward. I turned to look back at the minimart. The clouded window made it hard to see, but I could tell that Soula was at the glass door hugging Piccolo's cage and watching me go.

I concentrated hard as I drew four big letters in the fog on my window. I was careful to reverse them: H-E-R-O.

I hoped that Soula could see.

after the fire

"Dwight?" I cleared my throat and waited. Grandio stood nearby, waiting to take the phone.

"Addie? Is that you?"

"Yes. Sorry to call so early," I said. Grandio gave me a nudge.

"Everything all right?"

"Dwight, I burned down your trailer," I said.

"Sweet screamin' jeez— You all right?"

"Fine," I said.

"Denise okay?"

"She wasn't there."

Grandio huffed and mumbled. "Not there, all right!" I covered my ear, tried to block him out.

"Wow. So what happened?" Dwight asked.

"It was stupid. I'm really sorry. I was being stubborn. There was a pan on the stove and I—"

Grandio took the phone. "Dwight, this is Jack here. Yeah, they say—"

He told Dwight everything while I sat at the old farm table in my soggy bathrobe. Eventually, I tuned out. I picked through a shopping bag of stuff Mrs. Casey had given me. (She had come to the fire prepared.) There was a T-shirt, a sweatshirt and a pair of jeans, a 3-pack of underpants, some socks and a sports bra. I thought about some of the things that were gone now, lost in the burned trailer forever: a bank card—melted now; an electric blue duffel—incinerated; a vocabulary book— probably in ashes.

"Addie," Grandio held the phone out to me. "Dwight wants you back."

"Wants me back? Oh." I took the phone.

"Addie, I just want to make sure you know, the trailer means nothing. Nothing at all. All I care about is that you're okay. Got it?"

"Got it," I choked.

"Okay. We'll be down later tonight. All of us."

I set down the phone.

"Well, girl," Grandio said, "better go get your-self warmed up in the shower."

"Right," I said. "My second one today."

That night, everyone seemed to be in such good moods. Grandio was enjoying having a crowd to cook dinner for. Besides, he was mush in Hannah's presence, and she was helping him in the kitchen. The Littles climbed all over me. They asked about the fire and kind of inspected me as if there should be something visibly different about me after what had happened. Dwight was making jokes. "I don't care about the trailer," he said. "But you could have invited us over if you were going to have a bonfire. We could have roasted wieners and marsh-mallows, kid!"

The laughter made me relax. Soon the whole crazy day started to slip away like an old skin and all I felt was tired. I sank into the couch. Dwight would hardly leave my side, and I found myself lean-ing sleepily toward him—going for his arm again, the way I always used to. "Sorry," I said, righting myself on the couch beside him. He pulled me back over without a word and sat twirling a strand of my hair in his finger until they had to leave.

something familiar

Helena and her mom drove a big box of second-hand clothes out to Grandio's farm three days after the fire. The room mothers from my old school had taken up a collection. I say *old* school because now that I was living at Grandio's, I was being reenrolled at Borden again. My old school had become my new school and vice versa.

"Some of the stuff in the box is kind of lame," Helena whispered as she leaned toward me. "But some of it's good. Robert's older sister sent some things. She gets good stuff and I think it'll fit you."

I had about four minutes to show Helena around the farm. Her mother stood on the front step with Grandio, but they were shuffling their feet the whole time like people trying to think of something to say. I didn't have too much hope of seeing Helena again, but we both pretended that we would.

Meanwhile, I heard just bits and pieces about Mommers. I was pretty sure Mrs. Casey had figured me for a liar when I said I didn't know where Mommers was staying. But it was the truth. Heck, I didn't even know Pete's last name. But somehow they found her. Grandio told me that. He explained that she was not permitted to visit me just yet, and I think she might have even been taken to jail, at least for a while. I didn't ask. I knew that courts and agencies would make all the decisions. Mrs. Casey would come around when she had questions for me.

After supper that night, I talked to Grandio.

"I really miss Piccolo," I said. "And . . . um, I really think it's too much to ask Soula to keep on taking care of a pet when she isn't so well, ya know?"

He looked up from his paper. (He had a habit of reading at the table.) "Where we gonna put a mouse?"

"Hamster," I said. I got up from the table and set my dishes in the sink. "I'll keep her in my room," I promised.

Grandio scowled as he thought. I hooked my fingers into the belt loops of my Mrs. Casey jeans and waited for an answer.

"Those little rats are nocturnal. It'll keep you awake all night. How about we put her out in the barn or the coop? She'll like the straw," he suggested.

"Piccolo isn't used to that. She won't bother me at night. We shared a bunk in the trailer. She needs something . . . familiar. She needs me."

Grandio let a few seconds grind by. "Saturday, then. We'll pick her up."

I let my breath go.

the going-away note

"Hi ya, Elliot!" I made a grand entrance at the minimart like a celebrity returning to her stage. "I'm back for Piccolo. Grandio's running errands and says I've got forty-five minutes to visit. Where's Soula?"

Elliot's face was hanging sort of plain and expressionless. He gave me a weak smile and whispered, "We lost her, Addie."

I leaned forward. "You lost Piccolo?"

"No. We lost Soula."

"What? Elliot? You're joking, right?" I spoke slowly. "Like . . . uh . . . how could anyone lose something as big as Soula?"

"No, kiddo. I'm sorry. I mean she died."

It must have been me who screamed. I felt it in my throat. I rushed to the Greenhouse, sure I'd find her there in the papasan chair, shaking out a chuckle the way she did. All I found was the chair—empty, like a nest. All her things—all Soula's bright, crazy, colorful scarves and big dresses—hung still in the open closet. Her nail polish bottles—hot pinks and cherry reds—stood like little toys on the vanity. Elliot had come in behind me. He gave me a hug when I turned around.

"Was it because of me? Was it the fire?" I asked. "Did that day kill her?"

"No, no, no. She was just so sick," he said.

"Oh, Elliot. I can't believe it. I thought I'd come back and give her this humongous hug and . . ."

"I know," he said. "Addie, you should just let it out. The waterworks, I mean. You'll feel much better."

Boy, that was all I needed to burst the dam. Elliot opened me up a minipack of tissues.

"Here ya go." He handed them to me. "I've gone through at least ten of these myself and I'm not done yet. She's left a big empty spot in this poor heart." He thumped his chest.

I think I cried for everything that day. For Soula, for the fire, and for how much Elliot hurt. I cried for being mean to Dwight and for not being with him and my little sisters. I cried for Mommers and for not knowing what would happen to us all.

Later, Elliot poured me a hot chocolate and brought Piccolo over to me. I sat on a milk crate with the cage between my feet. Elliot sat on Soula's old busted-down lawn chair. We sat looking out across the street at the empty black patch where the trailer had stood. I could see the grassy slope that led up to the train. It was greening up with springtime almost like it was repairing itself.

"What happened to seven down and one to go?" I asked him.

"She never had the last one. To tell you the truth, I think the battle was over a while ago. But none of us wanted to say so."

I blew my nose and went for another tissue.

"Do you think it was those brown fields, Elliot? Is that how Soula got the cancer? Do you think it was the gasoline tanks?"

"We'll never know," he said, shaking his head. "No one can be sure. There are mysteries in life, kiddo. And some of them just plain stink. But you should know that when it came time, she really needed to go. She wanted to go. Oh, and she left you something!" He bounced up, went to the cash register, and pulled a fat envelope out of the drawer and handed it to me. I hesitated.

"Should I open it now?"

"Sure."

The bulk of it was money—a lot of green bills. I could just about see Soula's hands, her hot-pink nails slipping bills into that envelope. It made me dizzy to think about it. I didn't count the money. I was interested in a handwritten letter that was wrapped around it. I unfolded it.

> *Dear Cookie,*
>
> *I've got few regrets as I float out of here, but I sure am kicking myself for never asking you to play your flute for me. I always thought there'd be time for Addie Schmeeter's minimart debut. Then suddenly your flute was gone. I'm guessing there's a good reason for that.*
>
> *This isn't enough cash-ola for an expensive new instrument. But maybe there's a secondhander out there, or even something else that'll help you get your dreams back in order. You decide.*

Last thing, Cookie: If I made mistakes when it came to you and your well-being, I'm sorry. This heroism business doesn't come with instructions. We can only follow our instincts. I'm glad to have been one of your heroes, and glad that you were here on the corner being one for me.

Keep crossing bridges and poking your nose behind gates, Little Cookie. It's a big, big world.

Love, Soula

"Wow," I whispered. "She writes a great going-away note."

"Yes, she does," Elliot said. Then he laughed. "Listen to us! She's got us talking about her in the present tense."

For a moment, I did feel like Soula was still there.

Elliot promised to take me around to the music stores. "I think there's three hundred dollars there"—he gestured toward the envelope in my hand—"and nobody drives a harder bargain than yours truly. There's a flute in your future, kiddo. *If* that's what you want."

I lifted Piccolo out of her cage and let her tunnel up the sleeve of my sweatshirt. She turned around at my elbow and came back into my hand. It felt good to hold her tiny vibrating body, good to feel her take up some space. She looked up at me and blinked. I remembered Soula winking with her amazing lined eyes.

defining normal

Grandio didn't have much time for a sad story. He dished me up a double bowl of ice cream when we got home, but he didn't give me any pep talks about loss and death and dying. I didn't really blame him. Some things are too hard to talk about.

He was nice about Piccolo moving in; he let me take her upstairs. I kept very close track of Pic. I couldn't stand the idea of losing anything else.

Grandio took feeding me very seriously. He said that was part of his job as my agency-appointed guardian. But he always made long and heavy sighing sounds as he worked in the kitchen. I offered to cook but he wouldn't allow that. If I did anything more than set the table he stopped me, saying, "No, no, you sit down, girl. I'll get the supper out. I'll get it." His food was good, but every once in a while I craved one of my own toast dinners.

Grandio made me a paper bag lunch every day, and every day he slathered the bread with mustard and slapped two pieces of bologna inside. I didn't like mustard. I tried to tell him, but I guess Grandio thought that mustard went with bologna and that was that. Still, it was nice to find the lunch on the bench by the door every day as I headed out for the school bus. Something to count on. After a while I got used to mustard.

But I did *not* get used to the things Grandio had to say about Mommers. He would suddenly bring up bits about the old "abandonment charges." Then he let it drop that the new charges were called "child endangerment."

"How in heck does somebody forget to come home and take care of her own babies?" he'd say. Then he'd add something like "I got a yard full of idiot birds—chickens—that know better than that!" He'd shake his head. "Call it 'endangerment' or anything else ya want. That woman's a criminal!"

Criminal.

I swallowed hard.

. . .

I don't know what I expected as far as Mommers was concerned, but I am sure that I didn't expect to see the blue car come rumbling up to Grandio's farm. But one day in April, it did. I was standing on the picnic table filling the bird feeder that hung from the apple tree out in front of Grandio's house. Mommers got out of her car, but she left the door open like she wouldn't be staying long. She looked at me as if it'd been two years instead of five weeks since she'd seen me.

"Addie, baby," she said hoarsely. "Addie, can you believe all this?" She pushed her hand into her stringy hair and held it in a clawlike grip. Her sweater fell open and I could just make out the lump of the baby at her belly. "We were so close this time. If I'd just had a little more time to make the business work—" She stopped and shook her head.

I had no idea what to say to Mommers. Finally, I offered that I was sorry about the fire. The bird feeder squeaked as it swayed on the tree branch over my head, and I remembered how the train used to rock the trailer.

"No, don't be sorry about that old piece of junk," she said. She began to cry. "I'm sorry I was gone so—"

"Out!" Grandio boomed. He stood on the front step, one arm raised straight as a stick, pointing down the driveway. He held the phone in his other hand. "You're violating the order, Denise. One call. That's all I gotta make."

"Jack, don't! How can you—" She stopped and took a step toward him. She took a hard swallow and said, "I just want five minutes with my little girl."

Little girl?

Grandio shook his head. "Not while I'm standing here."

"Please, Jack! Don't . . . don't do this! Five minutes! Five." She held up her hand, fingers spread wide.

"Grandio," I said, "couldn't she just stay a minute? I know it's against all the decisions, but isn't anybody gonna ask me what I want?"

He finally nodded and stepped back into the doorway.

Mommers kept making little noises in her throat. She fussed with her hair and wiped at her nose with the back of her hand.

"So, how's Pete?" I asked.

She raised her eyebrows. "Pete is . . . well . . .

279

he's pretty flippin' surprised."

"Then he knows? About the baby?" I glanced at her belly.

"Yeah, he does now. He's going to try to help me, believe it or not!"

"I believe it," I said. "It's his kid."

Mommers nodded. "Pete and I have a lot to get past and we're just getting started. God, it's such a mess! They're gonna make me take *parenting* lessons. They think I won't know how to take care of the baby when he gets here."

"It's a boy?"

She nodded and pulled a ratty tissue from her pocket.

"Well, Pete can help, right?"

"I think so." Mommers nodded again and blotted her eyes. I spent a second imagining—hoping—that Pete, whoever he was, would be a really good dad—like Dwight. "What about you, Addie? How are you?"

I shrugged. "Grandio takes good care of me. I look fine, don't I?"

Mommers laughed and tears rolled down her cheeks. "Yeah! You do look fine. Have you seen my Brynna and my Katie?"

"Yes. They come often. Everyone was here for Easter," I said. "Brynna went home with purple sleeves from the egg dye. Katie wouldn't bite the ears off her chocolate bunny 'cause she said he wouldn't be able to hear without them."

"Oh, I miss them so much!" Mommers started to cry again.

"I know. Me too," I said. I wished I'd had fresh tissues for Mommers. She still had lots of crying to do and I knew how that felt.

"Did you hear about Soula?" I asked.

"Oh, yes. And I was so sorry," Mommers said. "Must have been awful."

"I miss her," I whispered. "She was really good to me."

"Yes, she was." Mommers nodded. She cleared her throat. "Addie, you said nobody asks what you want. Do you *know* what you want?"

"I just want . . . *normal*," I said.

"What's normal?" Mommers squinted at me. "Things are always changing. I mean, how does anyone know if they've got normal?"

I thought for a second. "I've felt close to it before," I said. "Normal . . . is when you know what's gonna happen next. Not *exactly* what, because probably nobody gets that. But *normal* is being able to count on certain things. Good things. And it's having everyone together—just because they belong that way." I realized I was making a circle with my hands as if I were holding on to a tiny world. "I keep waiting for it to happen to us," I said, looking up at Mommers. "But we—we never seem to get all the way to normal."

Mommers looked back at me blankly.

"Time's up!" Grandio shouted from the doorway.

Mommers got into her car quickly. Before she shut the door she said, "We'll get it someday, Addie. We'll get normal."

I know she meant that with all her heart, but as I watched the blue car bump away down Grandio's long driveway I didn't hold much hope. *All or nothing* never added up to normal.

Grandio launched a big long rant about Mommers that rose and fell all that afternoon and through our meat loaf dinner. "I could have made that call, I tell ya!" He filled one cheek with potatoes. "One hot second and I would have reported her. Taught her to respect the laws that—"

"Stop!" My own shout rang back at me. "I can't stand it if you keep going on about her! I can't!" I burned with tears and silence for the next few seconds. I expected him to shout back at me, but he didn't.

He finally ducked his head and mumbled, "You're right, girl. That's it. I'm done with it now."

Somehow, I knew he meant it.

full of surprises

All through the month of May, I got visits. Dwight and Hannah brought the Littles down to see me as much as three times a week. "You are here a lot," I said one day. "What about the work on the inn? And what about your wedding?" They just said they were budgeting time differently these days and that the wedding was on hold until some other things got worked out. At first, I was afraid they'd changed their minds about marrying. But they always walked in holding hands. I knew to watch Brynna, and I did. If anything were wrong, she'd be twisting her napkin. She seemed happier than ever.

I longed to go up to Lake George, but Youth and Family Services had me sort of captive, within a certain radius of Grandio's house. I could go places, but not far. I didn't ask questions.

Elliot and Rick took me to the mall one night and spoiled me rotten with french fries, root beer, bubble gum and a new CD player. While we were there, we put my name on a list at the music store. They'd call about any secondhand flutes that came in, but it might be a while. I ended up spending some of the Soula Flute Fund money anyway. I took half an hour to decide, but then I bought an Irish tin whistle. "I want something to play in the meantime," I told Elliot and Rick. "Someday, I'll be good enough to try a piccolo. This tin whistle will be pretty easy." I figured out part of my solo from "I Wonder as I Wander" before we even left the store.

"Wow! That's beautiful. How did you do that?" Rick asked.

"She's brilliant," Elliot told him.

I giggled into the whistle and made it squeak something awful. Heads turned. We left the mall in a fit of laughs.

Mrs. Casey made regular visits to the farm. We talked about everyone in my family, including the people I thought of as my family even if there wasn't a blood relationship.

"I want to live with my sisters and my . . . Dwight," I told her. I didn't care that it wasn't likely to happen, or that I was just a pebble in a big sea that would decide what to do with me. "We belong together," I insisted. I even tried to explain my idea of normal to her.

For all my rattling on and on, I felt like Mrs. Casey was wasting everyone's time. I'd end up with Mommers again somewhere down the line.

But there was one thing about Mommers that I'd forgotten to figure in: she was full of surprises.

In early June, when everything was quiet and nobody, including me, seemed to be clawing for anything at all, I looked up from where I was watering Grandio's new marigolds. I saw Dwight coming across the yard.

"Addie!" he called. "Addie! You won't believe this!" He fell right down on his knees about twenty feet in front of me. He reached into his back pocket and held a fat envelope up high.

"What's that?" I asked.

"Adoption papers!" His voice rang out. "You're mine! I'm yours!"

"We're *what*?" I dropped the hose. I took a step toward him.

Don't be a dream, don't be a dream.

"For real?" I asked.

"For real!" he said.

I ran to him—full speed ahead, arms open wide—and hit him hard. We both fell over in the grass.

Grandio found us a few minutes later. We were lying on our bellies, elbows linked. We had the papers spread out in front of us, and I kept sniffling and running my fingertips over the circular seals that'd been embossed into every page. It was *official*.

"What's with you two? You'll get bugs up your shirts," Grandio said.

"Three girls, Jack! I got three girls!" Dwight stood up and handed the papers to Grandio.

"Did you both know about this?" I asked.

"We've been working on it with your Mrs. Casey." Grandio grinned. "And so have you, girl, though you didn't know it! We didn't want to say anything until it really came through." He put his glasses on his nose and scanned the papers. "So

287

Denise did a good thing, by gosh! Signed, and with no stipulations!"

"That's Mommers," I said, wiping my face with my hands. "All or nothing." I fell back on the grass and watched the sky spin.

all to home

With just two weeks left until the start of summer vacation, we all decided together that it would make the most sense for me to finish out the year at Borden School. It was hard to wait, but it was also the first time I'd ever had the chance to get used to the idea of moving somewhere new.

I sat beside Dwight on the front seat of the pickup the day he drove me home to Lake George. I held Piccolo's cage on my lap and settled my palm into the spot where Soula's weight had bent the wires the morning of the fire. Dwight reached over and covered my hand with his. He gave me a grin and I matched it.

I knew I'd see Mommers again. Maybe someday she'd be allowed to bring her new baby to see her old babies. She *did* love us. I knew that, and I decided to look for a time to tell Brynna and Katie so. I wiped away a spill of tears, closed my eyes and remembered some of the times that Mommers had made me laugh.

Once off the highway, the truck wound along the old mountain road. I braced myself and held Pic's cage a little tighter as we took the last sharp turn that met the straightaway up to the inn. It made me laugh when I thought about it; I had come twisting and turning home.

Sunlight glowed across the new lawn and broke into a patchwork of shadows on the porch. Brynna and Katie came running out the open door, giggling and carrying a long banner that circled and blew back against their legs. I watched the roll of paper straighten out before me. In big painted letters with little handprints everywhere it read: ALL TO HOME ADDIE!

"All," I whispered to myself.

Then I hustled up to the porch to be with my sisters.

acknowledgments

With all my heart, I thank my family and my friends for keeping the net pulled taut beneath me. (You all know who you are.)

My special thanks to:
Jennie, for your unmatched energy.
Katherine, for your belief and your wisdom.
Emily, for braiding every end.

DATE			